Orbatz in the Everglades

Alex Cook

Clythe R. Bennett

ALEX COOK

outskirtspress

DENVER, COLORADO

Outskirts Press, Inc.
http://www.outskirtspress.com

ISBN: 978-1-4787-7200-2

Outskirts Press and the "OP" logo are trademarks belonging to Outskirts Press, Inc.

PRINTED IN THE UNITED STATES OF AMERICA

ACKNOWLEDGEMENTS

The editorial duty on this manuscript and the chauffeuring work of my special companion, and her company in visits to our favorite places in South Florida is most gratefully acknowledged. We have particularly enjoyed the accommodations and attention in Everglades City of the managements and staffs of the Ivey House and of City Seafood on the Barron tidal river just across the street. (I will always remember the prompt action of those ladies when the gust of wind blew my box of stone crab claws into the street.)

In my many years living in and visiting South Florida I have many memories of special nature spots in the days before habitat loss had diminished the birdlife, places like Everglades National Park, the Arthur R. Marshall Loxahatchee National Wildlife Refuge, Audubon's Corkscrew Swamp Sanctuary, and the J.N. Ding Darling National Wildlife Refuge.

Alex Cook

AUTHOR'S NOTE

This is a fictional story set for the most part in Everglades City in southwest Florida. My 50 years detailed familiarity with South Florida locations includes my 25 years residence in Boca Raton as Professor of Physics in the initial years of Florida Atlantic University. I made numerous visits to the Everglades, southwest Florida, and the Keys during my tenure at FAU, and have more recently made occasional visits from my atmospheric science research site in Colorado.

While many of the described events are typical for time and place, they are all completely fictional and bear no actual relationship to things past or present. Nova University is drafted as the fictional site for Orbatz' faculty and student positions. Similarly, descriptions of institutions, businesses, or natural sites are depicted as details and events necessary for the fictional story; departures from reality to fiction remain challenges for the reader.

Orbatz' website descriptions of climate change science are based on my research background and recent atmospheric science studies. These are not fiction. On the other hand, the weather events in the story are fictional but typical of South Florida. The extreme weather events are plausible results of Florida's business as usual policies. The Florida political responses and public apathy are real and dangerous and the sea level threats are troubling. Climate expert James Hansen has stated: "Sea level disaster ahead, but when?"

Table of Contents

PART I: STAGE SETTING 1
  Cargo for the Lady.. 3
  Orbatz Sabbatical 8
  Orbatz Curriculum Vita 13
  Professor Fairchild Retirement.......................... 17
  Everglades City 19
  Davie.. 47
  The Greenwich Lady...................................... 76
  The Glades Lady 80
  Colorado 99

PART II: ORBATZ AND CLIMATE CHANGE 103
  Orbatz' Website 114
    I. Everglades History 114
    II. Greenhouse Effect.................................. 120
    III. Global Warming.................................... 129
    IV. Solutions 137
    V. Climate Change 142

PART III: CLIMATE CORPS.................................... 147
  The Judge and the Senator 157
  Glades I Introduction 161
  Chokoloskee Turbine 178
  Congressman Beasley 183

Alice ··· 193

Orbatz' Website ································· 195

    VI. Protest ·································· 195

The Program ···································· 197

Glades II ··· 198

Glades III Policy Shift ······················ 206

Tesla I Introduction ························· 216

PART IV: LEADERSHIP ····················· 219

Carlos ·· 221

Glades IV Workshop ························· 226

Fishing ·· 231

Harold ··· 239

EPILOGUE ·· 245

Colorado ·· 247

Tesla II Transition ··························· 250

Simon ··· 253

ABOUT THE AUTHOR ······················· 257

PART I
STAGE SETTING

Cargo for the Lady

The interior of the Jamaican pub was dimly lit; a single fluorescent strip illuminated the bar. James, the barkeep, slowly polished glasses for early customers. The wall clock registered 4:15. A cage accommodating a large green parrot hung from the rafters just inside the entrance to the Mariner's Berth. Jay Whitmore, owner-captain of the Greenwich Lady, approached, dressed in a florid tropical shirt, white trousers, deck shoes, and battered captain's cap. He paused, lightly caressing the shoulder of the tall blonde in white halter and shorts, then opened the heavy door to the cool pub interior. With dark glasses perched on her head, the blonde stepped cautiously inside. The loud "HELLO" from the parrot stopped her in her tracks. Husband Jay stumbled away from the sound to avoid a collision, "It's a damn parrot! Say good day to the pretty bird, Abby."

The parrot continued, "I'm King George!"

"Good afternoon, George—and now I really do need a drink!"

Jay and Abby proceeded to the bar. James apologized for the startling welcome, "And a complimentary drink for the lady. We've got rum, rum, and more rum! I'm James, at your service."

Jay answered, "And we are the Whitmores from Greenwich, Connecticut. I'm Jay and this is Abby. We will start with your recommendation for a before-dinner drink—dining room open soon?"

"Yes, the ladies are making final preparations." James quickly brought drinks, "Our rum specialty." Stepping away, he lifted a wall phone for a brief message.

King George paused from his observations of the bar to scratch his head and prepare to greet a new customer. "Wipe your feet!"

The somewhat scroungy male paused while exchanging sunglasses for a large horn-rimmed pair. The cut-off jeans and grimy t-shirt suggested a local ne'er-do-well. He began to scuff his feet, and then said, "Cool it, George!"

Proceeding towards the bar, he exclaimed, "Hello Abby, Jay. Saw the Greenwich Lady at the dock. Thought you might be here!"

Abby gazed at the greeter with a puzzled expression. "Is that you, Harvey? What's with the get-up, the mustache, glasses, funny hat?"

Harvey cautioned with left forefinger raised. "You last saw me in the Mediterranean, in Athens, I believe." Then whispering, "Please, the DEA likes to keep tabs on me after busting me for growing pot a few years ago, remember?" After a cautious look around, he continued, "But I think our little arrangement to take some presents back to the folks in Greenwich worked out nicely—I thought you might like to help me out on another little project this time around. Say, those sparklers in Abby's ears look pretty classy, don't they, Jay?"

Jay grudgingly agreed, accompanied by a frown.

Harvey continued in a whisper, "And that project also helped top off the fuel tanks, didn't it! Now I have a proposition that will be hard to refuse. Care to move another $100K into the Cayman account?"

"Look, Harvey, I made some fancy moves at the bank a couple of years ago that were just barely legal. No point in going over the line at this stage." The boat captain paused to sample his rum. "Cash flow is a little tight, though. We really splurged on some things in Greece and Italy."

Harvey replied in a whisper, "OK. Here's the deal. You have a first class reputation and a boat that's not the sort that will generate suspicion. And you must be on the up-and-up to rub elbows with the folks in Connecticut. My new friends would like to borrow your cover to transfer a big bundle of pleasure into the States. Just a ride for a package in your boat—no involvement by you at all—just normal visits at the best marinas as you head for home. The DEA won't expect anything from a motorsailer like yours at those topflight marinas. They spend their time looking for run-down fishing boats in the mangroves."

"Well—"

"Now here's the plan—"

King George cocked his ears for remarks that might yield a goody from the bar. Mumbles were faint, though, to hinder any interest by the barkeep.

"A stopover at Cozumel on about May 8-15. You will always enjoy dinner ashore. Some time in that period you will get delivery of about 10 life saving cushions—and some valuable plastic bundles stashed away behind some panels in the cabin. You don't need to know or think about it. The cushions will be your signal to depart for Key West about May 18-25. There you will check out the arty-type museums and watch the sunset show at Mallory Square and have dinner ashore each evening. And some evening you will take delivery of a supply of Jack Daniels—signaling relief of your cargo—and you will find a package of $50K in your freezer. You will patiently wait until the merchandise is deemed satisfactory for payment. When that decision is made, you will get radio confirmation of your reservation for a sport fishing date on the Caribbean Pirate at Cozumel. While you are out looking for sailfish, you will find another packet of $50K and a delivery of Tanqueray to signal completion of the project. Then a leisurely trip back to Greenwich and your usual method of transferring $100K to the account in the Caymans."

Broward County Commissioner Cerwinski was expecting visitors. The Bacardi bottle in the right hand file drawer was the reserve supply for the brownish liquid in the glass nestled suggestively near the can of Coke. His secretary announced the arrival of the prominent developer Abraham McDonald and his well-dressed friend, Paolo Brinelli. The developer extended a well-manicured hand. "Ah, Commish, your political support chairman wishes you well. How are all your irons in the fire this sunny May morning? I suspect you have a few budget problems as always, but I'm sure your Foundation for Unwed Mothers must be getting some flattering attention. Perhaps our conversation will improve your outlook on some of these things."

"Don't I wish! Or are you bringing me more problems?"

"Heaven forbid! We've come to solve your problems. But you could help us with this townhouse development we have planned for that area out near the levee west of Davie. My companion, Paolo, is expecting a substantial investment to accrue from his import and distribution network. It should be good for a few dozen townhouses, a pretty little lake from the fill excavation, a putting green for the old duffers, and an exercise walk for the ladies; just like the plans we forwarded to you last week. Should raise a few mill in taxes!"

"Ah, yes. But you are aware that this fellow Orbatz has been working with Audubon to preserve that swamp for some little brown bird? I think it's called a sora rail."

"Not a problem! We'll construct feeding stations outside the bedroom windows for the little fellows to sing to the old folks in the morning."

The commissioner sat with pursed lips studying the photograph of Panther Stadium. "I somehow wonder if Audubon will expect this bird to do that sort of thing."

Brinelli interrupted, "Well, whatever. I'm sure you can work out some arrangement. Perhaps you can persuade this Orbatz to take his bird problem and shove it some place where the sun doesn't shine! And I'm sure your secretary can advise us of a procedure for granting a few hundred thou to your foundation. We won't occupy any more of your valuable time. Have a good day!"

Orbatz Sabbatical

It was Monday morning, the 27th of May. The air was balmy; a few cumulus appeared but no storms were brewing. End of term reports were finished with no complications. The letter was written and accepted. Sabbatical conditions were in order; no duties were pending. Professor John Orbatz lived in a furnished one-bedroom rental apartment; rent was paid until the lease would expire next month. Elizabeth had kept the house in Davie after the divorce. The professor's natural reaction was to prolong his morning coffee, put his feet up, and read the Sun-Sentinel. Then contemplate his navel, so to speak. The watchers would expect that.

The cell phone contact had occurred promptly at 2 AM, as scheduled. And the small duffel with the laptop, research papers, casual clothes, and other necessities had been stashed in the trunk of the old Toyota at 3 AM. Breakfast dishes were stacked in the sink. A week's worth of underwear and socks plus a towel or two were in the spin cycle of the washer. The bed was just as he had crawled out of it three hours earlier. There was a total of $10,000 in $100 bills in his money belts.

A quick stop at Walgreens was appropriate: he might need a generous stock of allergy medicine sometime in the future. But first came a requisite study of the situation under the hood of the Toyota and a check for fluid under the car, although a repetition of the brake failure from a broken hydraulic line was unlikely. The car problems had been infrequent and low key—but a warning. The firebomb through the bedroom window was luckily a dud but it was apparent that somebody didn't like him very much. A few other errands would set the stage, then the trip to the Ft. Lauderdale airport. Wearing standard professorial attire of corduroy jacket, bow tie, slacks, and loafers, he checked in for the Frontier flight to Denver well in advance of the 2 PM departure; his duffel was carry-on. He posted the letter containing title to the Toyota and parking stub to his secretary; she already had a key. Then he purchased a copy of an early story of the adventures of Doc Ford, and relaxed with a small pizza.

Twenty minutes later, Orbatz made a preparatory stop in the Men's Room on the way to the Security lines. The jacket was abandoned on a hook in the toilet, the bow tie disappeared, the slacks and shoes were carefully stowed away in the carry-on, and a casually dressed tourist in Bermuda shorts and Nike running shoes ignored the Security lines to board the airport bus to the Hollywood central station. As on numerous earlier occasions, he had not been able to identify any representatives of the various groups that had inclination to do him mischief or bodily harm. Still, this trail of confusing intent might be useful in avoiding any close pursuit. In Miami, he boarded the 1:10 bus to Key West.

In Key West, John Orbatz made his way from the bus terminal to the small Conch Friends bar near the waterfront on Florida Bay. He observed his fellow customers with some care as he indulged in an early dinner of steak and Florida lobster. He became content that there was no imminent discovery or danger. A crisp 10-dollar bill convinced the barkeep to be amenable to temporary custody of his duffle. Then, free to wander about as a tourist, he was able to purchase the standard hat and sunglasses to possibly pass as a Conch Republic native. Passage of time was tedious, though, and he moved to join in the sunset celebration at Mallory Square. There were country singers and bluegrass. There was an escape artist swathed in chains. There were fortunetellers and magic tricks, and a bleary-eyed drunk attempting to do card tricks. Orbatz' companions in the audience, a smartly dressed couple—a boat captain and his blond companion—recognized the alcoholic symptoms of the fiasco. Orbatz was about to turn away when he heard, "Been there, Friend. Take this bill and get a decent dinner and sober up." Then, shaking his head and removing his boat hat to wipe his brow, commented in an aside to Orbatz, "He's pretty far gone, but I understand it's the thing to do in Key West. Oh, we're the Whitmores from Connecticut. I wonder, would you care to follow the custom and join us for a beer at Hemingway's Sloppy Joe?"

Orbatz hesitated, then said, "Sorry, a bit slow—just an absent minded college professor. My name is John. I have a few minutes to kill—glad to visit with you over a cold one."

As they imbibed at the bar, there were additional informal introductions, "I'm Jay; this is Abby. We just arrived from Cozumel a few days ago; made the tour up and down Duval St. and enjoyed good seafood on the bay at the Conch Republic last night. Been sightseeing here, have you?"

Orbatz replied with casual falsehoods. "Oh, yes. Visited the Audubon House and the Hemingway House like everyone else. I highly recommend both."

"I suppose we should do that—maybe next trip. We're expecting a radio message from a friend in Cozumel to return there for charter fishing for billfish. Something new for us: are you an expert?"

"You're joking. Not on a college professor's salary. And speaking of which, I have a consultant appointment in a few minutes. But best of luck for sailfish or whatever!"

In early twilight, the casually dressed lady of Cuban descent strolled leisurely with her Jack Russell Terrier along the Key West waterfront. A young clean-shaven crew-cut male wearing a Penn State sweatshirt made a slight adjustment to his backpack and gave the lady a soft, polite greeting, "Nice evening for a walk—enjoy!" Then, ascertaining that he had no observers, he moved quickly down the dock towards berths 20 – 30.

Orbatz moved quickly away from Sloppy Joes and returned to the Conch Friends to retrieve his duffle. Then he casually approached the marina and wandered slowly toward the non-descript motorsailer in berth 23. He paused with a quiet "Hello, the boat; permission to board?" There was the tentative bark of a small dog; then he heard the whisper, "Yes, John!"

John Orbatz disappeared into the cabin below deck. All was quiet for a few minutes, and then there was an excited whispered conversation. Soon a cork popped from a bottle and the subdued conversation continued. Then more quiet, except for slight rustle of bedclothes.

At 4 AM, the Glades Lady left berth 23, and, with idling motor, moved at low speed into the bay. By sunrise, the sail was up and the boat was underway northward in the light easterly breeze.

At 10 AM a similar motorsailer, the Greenwich Lady, departed Key West for a sport fishing engagement at Cozumel.

Orbatz Curriculum Vita

Dr. John Orbatz, Professor of American Studies at Nova University, specialized in South Florida history. Although he was not widely recognized as an authority in this field, his long experience as an observer of events in the Florida economy and environment had secured a consulting agreement with the CIA. His advice concerning Cuban events had been contrary to the dedication of his neighbors in Little Havana and the less than efficient cooperation of Washington officials. Both groups were distressed with the turn of events in the Bay of Pigs and were independently determined to reward Orbatz as a presumed traitor. In addition to this difficulty, his scholarly publications and classroom lectures had left no doubt of his attitude toward Big Sugar's exploitation of the Everglades and the suburban developers' conversions of the natural habitat into forests of condominiums and wall-to-wall luxury houses encroaching from the Intracoastal westward towards the levee of the protective fresh water impoundments. And his warnings at Town and Gown meetings about a need to respond to global warming were an annoyance to the politicians and their supporting developers. He had a number of powerful enemies.

Publications of Orbatz' criticisms of the Bay of Pigs operation were widely circulated. The military aspects of the operation were a disaster, influenced greatly by the choice of invasion site. Air cover support was hamstrung by U.S. politicians' efforts to appear neutral and unaware of the project.

Secrecy was negligible; military training and preparations in Florida and elsewhere were well known. Orbatz' concluding consulting communications were flavored by the flawed haphazard preparations and by the clear strength of the Castro revolution. The CIA interpretations of these messages were that Orbatz had been complicit in the breakdown of secrecy. He was suspected of Communist leanings and subsequently branded as a card-carrying Communist to the University administration. His tenure application was denied and his scholarly efforts bad-mouthed by naive faculty members.

Orbatz' students exhibited an international flavor, many of Cuban descent. Some were clearly well educated and nicely integrated into the wealthy structure of Miami. Although friendly to their professor, they were well aware of his familiarity with Cuban history. The student grapevine had spread fragments of his CIA connection and he was viewed as an obstacle to any return to a pre-Castro era. Others were sullen in their acceptance of the status quo and would have welcomed Castro's downfall and Orbatz' demise by any means, including covert action. While the class work of this group was generally satisfactory, some were deficient in English communication and earned below average grades. They were less than happy with their instructor. There were a few optimists, however, who imagined a future political situation of constructive relations with the Cuban people.

The Army Corps of Engineers' early efforts to open the Florida Everglades to agriculture had been partially successful. The flow of surplus water from central Florida was channeled and diverted by numerous canals from Lake Okeechobee to the Atlantic. A related effect of the canal network was the opening of the area just west of the coastal ridge to row crop farming, followed by housing developments. But in dry seasons there was the surprising consequence of saltwater intrusion from the ocean into the aquifers and well water of the coastal communities. The solution was a large area of fresh water impoundments along the eastern edge of the true Everglades. This fresh water pressure served to protect the wells and to encourage the subsequent development from vegetable fields to urban areas.

But the final bonanza for the exploitation of the deep muck of the central Everglades was the Cuban sugar embargo. The potential of sugar cane had been recognized much earlier, and the subsidies for this industry in the absence of Cuban sugar opened the muck to lucrative profits. The South Florida Water Management District system of canals guaranteed dependable water for this industry as well as for urban development to the east.

But the easterly developments were becoming shy of open land, and the muck of the Everglades had become shallow and bereft of nutrients. The continued pressure of wealth from the Northeast and Midwest was an attractive incentive for continued development. There were thoughts that the levees of the fresh water impoundments could be relocated westward or Big Sugar could release its marginal land to development. And there was the Everglades Restoration Project, of course. Steps to reclaim the under-water scam developments of the western Everglades were well under way. But the State and especially Federal financial efforts in the east central Glades were foundering.

Orbatz had recognized the dual nature of the restoration

project. True, the restoration of fresh water flow into Everglades National Park had some support, but this was clearly not going to be allowed to the detriment of the eastern developments or at the expense of Big Sugar. Orbatz' analysis of the situation was making its way into the environmental movement. In addition, the appearance of the IPCC report of the human causes of global warming did little to shield Orbatz from the wrath of the business-as-usual establishment. Both the developers and Big Sugar would be happy to see Orbatz disappear from the Florida scene.

Professor Fairchild Retirement

I'm not really much of a party person, but this was a little bit special. My letter of resignation had been accepted; I was an early-retired professor of American History at age 55. My colleagues at Golden West University had honored me with a retirement dinner. I would no longer be observed shuffling off to teach a class every Monday, Wednesday, and Friday, or presiding at the all-college faculty meeting at the beginning and end of term. My absence at that ceremony would be a disappointment to many— although not to everyone, I suspected.

Our department chair had just finished a rather dry summary of the academic history of that seedy looking Professor Fairchild. Yours truly could do with a haircut and a new bowtie, I know. My office mate was jostled awake by his wife; he applauded a bit too vigorously and muttered the obligatory, "Speech; speech". As I struggled to my feet, I made the automatic search in coat pocket for my class notes—panic—no preparation for the first—and last—lecture.

"Unaccustomed to speaking—no, that won't work will it? I'm delighted to see so many shiny faces waiting for words of wisdom. Is that better? Not really: I see some faces that have more wrinkles than mine. And some that doubt that age has made me wise." I continued in this vein for perhaps ten minutes or so until the smiles began to fade and feet were shuffling about. "OK. I see that dessert is about to be served. Be it known that the registrar has my class grades. My desktop is clean for the first time in years. Bags are packed. The Prius has a new coat of wax. I'll be on the road to Everglades City on Monday morning. Take care of the store while I'm gone, won't you?"

My colleagues stopped for a handshake and 'Wish you well'. Most of the younger faculty had baby-sitters or additional important social engagements—or both. I was pleasantly surprised when our young first year Assistant Professor Albert Jensen and his pretty wife Amy made a concerted effort to break into the huddle. After the expected greeting, Amy asked, "Did I hear correctly that you will be spending time in a place called Everglades City? Isn't that in southwest Florida?"

I replied, "Yes, I've rented a small apartment there for a few months. I'll soak up some sun and begin to think about what I should do when I grow up."

Albert smiled briefly and added, "Amy's stepfather is Professor of American Studies at Nova University on the Florida east coast. We just had a thought that there might be some occasion for you to cross paths with him. Nothing special—but we will e-mail some contact information in a few days, if you don't mind."

"'Course not, although I have no plans to get into the rat race over there. Everglades City is a quiet little fishing town where I'll begin collecting information on the history of that region, like the Calusa Indians and Marjory Stoneman Douglas' *River of Grass*."

While their approach had been studiously casual, I sensed a serious side to it, particularly in Amy's approach and facial expression. I had no inkling of the search that would ensue.

Everglades City

A week later I had begun to settle in to the arrangement in Everglades City. The cross-country trip had been uneventful, a boring series of Interstate runs and Best Western stopovers until my arrival in North Florida. Then there was a more leisurely drive along the Florida west coast. I spent the first day at St. Marks National Wildlife Refuge with liberal use of my binoculars and spotting scope for documentation of wading birds on my digital camera. Following another stop at Cedar Key for a seafood dinner, I spent the night at the historic bed and breakfast. Then, after a compulsory visit to the fresh water springs and manatee in Wakulla Springs, I bypassed the circus museum and art museum in Saratoga might have to check into that sometime later. And finally a 2-day layover on Sanibel with a couple of late afternoons at Ding Darling and the opportunity to walk the beach early each morning to check for seashells at low tide. Little luck— too much competition from dozens of little old ladies in sun suits and flip-flops. So I lathered up with sunscreen and sunbathed on the sand.

The exit south from highway 41, the Tamiami Trail, onto 29 was an entry into an earlier South Florida Everglades world. The light local traffic was a welcome departure from all the frantic hustle of the early part of my trip. Scenery was restricted to a tangled mangrove forest along the adjacent canal—probably used as fill for the road. Suddenly there was an elevated bridge over a narrow waterway and I had arrived in Everglades City.

A slow crawl of a 10 block loop past the city center with historic buildings, museum, tennis courts, and the necessary motels and restaurants, returning along the tidal waterway with its several commercial fishing operations, and I had toured the northern half of the town. The realtor's office was an obvious welcoming establishment. My insistent ring at the front desk brought a pleasant lady from a rear patio to attend to my needs. "Good afternoon; I'm Mae Ellen Baker. May I help you?"

"Yes, I'm Russell Fairchild, just arrived from Colorado. I spoke with you a few weeks ago about the rental apartment on 3rd street."

"Oh, yes. I trust you had a pleasant journey. I have your Master Card deposit. If you like, we can check out the apartment now. I think we have it ready for you."

"That would be good. I hope it lives up to your description and pictures. I'm planning to be there for a couple of months' relaxation."

On 3rd St. I was shown the elevated one-bedroom apartment. Ground floor housed the A/C and a storage facility adjacent to the carport under a small deck. Above, the furniture was immaculate modern in an open living-dining area adjacent to a small gleaming white kitchen.

I exclaimed, "Nice! This appears to be completely new and unused."

"That's true. The owner purchased the property several years ago as an investment for his future retirement. Then, with advice from an interior decorator, added the new furniture.

The 32"TV is on cable and there is a complete stereo system in the cabinet there. The large bedroom has a queen size bed and a standard bath with shower. I thought you might like it," she finished with a smile.

"Yes I think so. And you said something about a dock near-by for a small boat."

"Yes, there is a short canal there off the main waterway, the Barron River. There will be weekly housekeeping services and linen exchange. Lawn service takes care of the small plots around these villas. Let us know if you have any other needs."

"Oh, I will. But don't expect any problems."

"Yes, this is a cut above most of Everglades City. It's good you arranged early in the summer. Most of our rentals are gone by late fall. This one is a bargain compared to the others. You have it for the summer but we'll have to check with the owner for later; he frequently spends a month or so here around Christmas."

"I neglected to bring groceries. What do you recommend?"

"We have a supermarket—sort of. Choices are limited but satisfactory. There are some larger shopping malls on the Trail west of here."

"And restaurants?"

"Everglades Rod and Gun Club is my choice. Dinner and cocktails on the patio along the waterway: pricey, but worth it. There are several others, of course; we get a few fishermen this time of year and quite a few tourists in winter. For breakfast, you could try the Oar House or the Ivey House. The Ivey is an old established bed and breakfast, popular with tourists and locals alike. The A/C and refrigerator are on. Your key, sir. Enjoy!" She turned to leave, but abruptly stopped to exclaim, "Oh, I hope you are aware of our swamp angels—salt marsh mosquitoes and no-see-ums. I don't recommend sitting on your deck after dark."

After moving the Prius into the carport, I proceeded to transfer all my stuff into the living room. No point in attracting the attention of enterprising thieves. Nothing was visible, so there was no excuse for violating the Prius. Then I found the PBS channel for Evening News featuring the same folks as in Colorado. Nice!

My realtor lady left me a map of the city—all 14 blocks—and I made my way to the Everglades Rod and Gun Club for my first taste of luxury in the Everglades. A celebratory dinner was called for. Time enough in days to come to conserve on my TIAA retirement. I had no problem finding a parking space for the Prius behind the impressive 2-story wooden building. Half a dozen stairs were required for access to the first floor. It was evidently common practice to anticipate an occasional few feet of floodwater, whether from a frog-strangler downpour or from the forefront of a late summer hurricane storm surge making its way up the tidal river through the mangroves. The large sign appeared to have been recently abbreviated, whether from a strong gust of hurricane force wind or perhaps to intentionally acknowledge that the establishment was no longer an exclusive club for wealthy sportsmen. The small sign near the back door warned that proper attire was expected and another warned that cash was required for dinner or accommodations, no credit cards.

The narrow entrance hall exhibited an impressive and

complete history of news clippings and photographs of notable visitors and residents, from the founding fathers to U.S. Presidents from Coolidge to Eisenhower. Additional evidence of their exploits at the expense of animals killed by high caliber weapons was exhibited. There was also documentation of the town's survival of frequent natural disasters involving strong winds and high water as well as a few disasters caused by human carelessness. A yellowed article illustrated the early Florida conservation activities of the Craighead family, familiar to me from their later studies of grizzly bears in my Rockies. Having absorbed a token amount of the history, I stepped into the exceptionally well-maintained high-ceilinged lobby area. An immense alligator adorned the wall overlooking the billiard table with balls available but silent. A black bear skin occupied the adjacent wall in company with the reptile. A stuffed bobcat perched on the shelf above the door to the adjacent bar, temporarily dark and quiet. I strolled carefully across the polished dark wood floor past the immense open fireplace and approached the small front lobby. An elderly lady behind the cluttered desk was making entries in a large registration book after working the lever of the mechanical calculator. My interest in the menu at the entrance to the large screened porch inspired no reaction from her. A huge fish with large scales above the dining room entrance was flanked by respectable samples of smaller fish that were probably not related to South Platte carp. I interrupted the lady at the desk; she recited tarpon, snook, and redfish without a glance.

The formal dining room was deserted, but somehow something was familiar about it. Ah! It was completely full in the movie *Gone Fishin'*. But the screened patio with the view of the tidal river looked more attractive now, occupied only by a casually dressed trio of middle-aged men at a distant table with their drinks poised, conducting a quiet conversation. They gave token observation to the Boston Whaler making slow progress up the Barron River against the outgoing tide. As I considered the expanse of tables with spectacular views of the river and westering sun, a waitress moved from the kitchen area across the empty dining room with a menu and table setting. A welcoming smile, and, "That table has your name on it, and the view couldn't be any better. Perhaps you'd like an afternoon cocktail to enjoy before dinner."

I agreed, "Yes, thank you. I'd like a Tanqueray on the rocks—no vermouth."

The quiet was broken only occasionally by the rustle of the wind in the palms on the narrow lawn by the river. The mumble of voices from the other table was my only reminder of other humans. The menu was challenging. My attitude for celebration was somewhat tempered by budgetary constraints. That is perhaps putting it on an overly organized basis. Nevertheless, I quickly eliminated the steak/lobster from consideration. I finally arrived at the catch of the day. I wonder if I should have been impressed to learn it was grouper.

I sat back to enjoy the view as I awaited my drink. The gently waving palms and outgoing tide occupied my attention; the reddening sun filled the sky along with a few mare's tail cirrus. A few of the motel customers began to fill the adjacent tables. I sipped my gin just as the slack tide welcomed a tall-masted vessel cautiously approaching the pilings a stone's throw from my table. The slender woman with tousled gray hair remained at the wheel as she monitored the activities of her young crewmembers securing the lines and hosing the deck.

My salad had just appeared when the new arrivals moved on to the patio to occupy one of the larger tables. One of the local gents promptly commented, "That's a fine looking sailboat. Been out in the Gulf, have you?"

The husky blonde guy nearest the questioner answered, "Yes, she's the 40 ft Wonderland, bound for the Pacific. Our lady captain has set the keyboard world straight with her computer science textbook and has finished her exploratory sailing of the Atlantic. We plan to enjoy New Zealand waters while you have your winter."

Another voice from the next table volunteered, "That should be a pleasant voyage. Give my regards to the Maoris and Kiwis on the North Island; I'm sure you'll find the natives are friendly."

And that ended the conversation between tables. The young crewmembers were studying the menu with advice from their captain and discussing the morning schedule and departure with the tide.

Next day, after a token breakfast of coffee, orange juice, and cereal, I resolved to begin the habit of a leisurely stroll along the tidal river. An early morning shower had left a few puddles in the potholes and the few remnant cumulus clouds were dissipating. The houses along River Street ranged from the modest wooden structures of a bygone era to large modern trophy homes. Nearly all were equipped with relatively new powerboats on hoists along the seawall of the Barron River.

There was little boating activity, however. I suspected that the weekend might bring a few fishermen out from their profitable business activities in the Naples area, or semi-retired families out for a pleasure boat ride. Further up the tidal river the scenery changed to commercial fishing. Numerous crab traps lined the seawall with an occasional workboat hitched to the pilings. Finally I came to a few seafood markets with signs proclaiming stone crab claws to be a specialty. A few appeared to serve seafood lunches in a modest setting of picnic tables. That might be an interesting alternative to my usual chicken soup and bologna sandwich. The Everglades City School had considerable playground activity; a fleet of yellow buses suggested this was a center for much of Collier County. But I wondered—looks just like the Ochopee School in the movie *Just Cause* with Sean Connery. And I wish that I could find a copy of *Wind Across the Everglades* with Burl Ives and Christopher Plummer, the story of Guy Bradley, the Audubon warden murdered by bird poachers. I understand it was also filmed here in Everglades City.

As I circled it to loop a return to my digs, I noticed a large rambling one-story building with parked cars and signage: The Ivey House. A few locals were arriving on bicycles. Ah, yes. I remembered the recommendation of breakfast at the Ivey House. I joined the trickle of locals to check out the possibilities for future mornings. The entrance suggested a rather new establishment—not the modern plastic of a Denny's, however. The atmosphere of wall and ceiling decoration was a neat replica of old Florida. Breakfast was evidently cafeteria style with community style seating—choose your companions. As I hesitated, having already eaten, the lady monitoring some activity on a computer asked, "Can I help? Would you care for breakfast?"

"Ah, but I've already eaten—can't do justice to all that food. Perhaps tomorrow."

"Good. Help yourself to a cup of coffee and we'll see you then."

I carried coffee to a table near the edge of the activity, and was quickly joined by a local couple. The lady in modest casual dress noted, "I see that Bertha has offered you a free sample. That will make you a regular in a hurry. I believe you just arrived in the Prius to rent Adam Thomson's apartment."

"Yes, very true. I guess things are quickly common knowledge in your small town."

Her companion asked, "Here for a bit of relaxation, are you?"

"Right. Here from Colorado to escape the end of winter. It's mud season."

"Well it's a quiet place except for a few commercial fishing boats in the early morning and evening. Unfortunately the tourist airboats take up the slack, especially on weekends. You'll find your way around soon enough. Try Island Seafood across the street for lunch later."

"This Ivey House is a surprise. Looks to be an old established place from the outside. Looks new inside."

"Yes, this section is new. Down the hall you'll find modern motel units with all the amenities, around a nice pool. The old lodge the other way has small bedrooms with the bath at end of the hall. It used to be the lodge for workmen building the Tamiami Trail, run by Mrs. Ivey.

"It's a busy place, good food too, I see. I'll be here tomorrow. Perhaps I'll see you again."

Come lunchtime, the sky was a startling blue; there were

a few clouds maturing for an afternoon shower. To avoid a sweat and sunburn, I decided to use the Prius to visit the Island Seafood for lunch. Parking in the street, though—tourists had arrived, possibly waiting their turn for airboat rides. Standing in the short line gave me ample time to select the conch chowder for lunch. The small kitchen and service area was busy with several ladies of varied stature and ethnicity. Still, I was startled to be giving my order to a pair of hazel eyes a few inches above my level. The eyes were bold and business-like. They said, "Let's get on with your lunch order. We're in too much of a rush to engage in pleasantries of weather and the like. And if you are inspired to comment on what a big girl I am, you just might lose your turn in line!"

I got the message, but it was a little disheartening. Not a real sociable outlook on life. "A bowl of conch chowder, please, and a Coors Light if you have it."

"That will be $6.25. Pick up your beer from the cooler behind you. Your chowder will be at the window to your left. You are number 41; listen for it. Next!"

Ah well. Business was a bit rushed; best be satisfied with the food without the pleasantries. After collecting my Coors and conch chowder, I moved to an empty picnic table in the sunshine. I continued my Colorado habit of solar exposure in spite of the 85° temperature and 79% humidity. Anyway, my floppy hat and sunscreen would protect me from that nasty UV-B. A small flock of about a dozen ring-billed gulls were hovering at attention in case a tourist was inclined to ignore the warning 'Feeding the birds may get you shat upon!' The brown pelican at eye level on the piling was similarly alert for any scraps of grouper being returned to the Barron River.

I made leisurely work of the chowder, with an eye on the tourist airboats and the occasional small outboard cruising in from the Gulf. As I continued to nurse my beer, I noted that the tourist crowd had thinned considerably. I was in no rush, however, and began to ponder on some trivial activity for the afternoon. I had not arrived at any inspiration when the tall kitchen person walked slowly to the edge of the pier while carefully spooning her bowl of lunch break chowder. As she slowly approached my location, I casually suggested "Happy to share my table if you like. Please, take a load off your feet."

"Oh yes, if you don't mind. We've had a busy time inside." The greeting continued to be impersonal. "Hope you're enjoying the chowder." Her not quite blonde hair was in some disarray, anchored in a bushy ponytail. Face had a liberal scattering of freckles. Skin was smooth but clearly showing signs of exposure to sun and wind. Hand and arms were similarly tanned—no jewelry, particularly no left finger ring, I noted. She continued to wear the slightly soiled white apron. I was quite interested to note that it failed to obscure the curves of a well-developed mature female. I lost interest in the river traffic.

I finally made a grocery run to the Crossroads Mall on the next weekend; it was about ten miles west on the Trail. I had given some care on my list to remember a need for cranberry juice for defense against the bugs in my bladder but found that I had failed to support Florida's principal food business: I arrived back in Everglades City with no orange juice! So next morning I pumped up the fat tires on my rental bike and breezed over to the local market. There I found Florida Friendly Fresh-squeezed Lots-a-Pulp for only a buck more than Minute Maid. I wondered, did lots-a-pulp come at the expense of the pure stuff? Or did the no pulp just have more Biscayne Aquifer water in it? I could probably use that extra fiber for my gut.

At the register I waited patiently for the blonde cashier to ring up an assortment of groceries and kitchen supplies, including Quaker Oats, Glades sugar, toilet paper, dish soap, and low fat milk. The customer was a short, rather stocky lady with dark hair showing traces of gray. Her eyes were lively, her smile happy, and her olive skin suggested Cuban heritage to my Midwest experience. There was some sort of conversation that suggested a need to leave toilet paper, cereal and dish soap for a later trip. Evidently the basket on her bike outside lacked space for the full load.

So, a reasonably attractive female in distress inspired my feeling of community. "I have a bike parked near yours with basket enough to help with your groceries. May I help and save you a trip?"

For answer I got a careful visual appraisal, then an abrupt "Thank you, sir, but No!"

Ah well. My cocktail bar technique for pick-up needed some modification for the checkout line! To the cashier, I remarked, "Just being neighborly."

She was sympathetic, "Luisa is really a nice lady—awfully suspicious of strangers, though. Seems especially nervous since her long trip out in the Gulf last month."

Since the bike tires still had plenty of air, I thought to swing by the seafood market for some fresh fish for evening dinner. Might be good to get there before the tourists.

Krista recognized me from my previous lunch visit. With a quick smile, "Good morning, Mr. Fairchild, I believe."

"Yes, but it's Russell, please—if I may call you Krista like on your little name tag? Could you suggest a choice of fish for dinner? I take it these are fresh from yesterday's trip to the Gulf."

"Certainly! One of those mutton snapper filets would be best. Probably enough for lunch or dinner tomorrow as well."

"Good! Probably worked out for the best to come down on the bike. I volunteered to help a local lady with groceries but got a polite refusal. I think her name was Luisa. Know her?"

"Oh, yes. She and her husband came from Cuba about ten years ago. They ran a party boat for tourists. He died a few years ago. She still makes a few trips, mostly for her previous clients."

"I was just being friendly, but she seemed suspicious. Hope I don't always come on that way, do I?"

Krista had an understanding smile. "'Course not. But I think Luisa already has a gentleman friend living with her. Sorry!"

Krista was a single mother with a 12-year old son, Daniel. Her husband had chosen a path at odds with Krista's dedication and the divorce had become official in Daniel's first year of life. He had little recollection of his father, who now had an address at an institution in North Florida. Krista's work hours ended at 4:30 to permit her to meet Daniel at the school in her old Chevy truck. Daniel and several of his friends made good use of that hour after school, usually in perfecting their soccer expertise.

On the afternoon following the conversation about mutton snapper with Russell at the market, Krista's phone rang as she entered her small 2-bedroom house near the road to Chokoloskee. "Hi Krista. It's me, your female sea-faring friend. Do you have a few minutes to visit? I wonder if you might be able to satisfy my curiosity about a small personal matter."

"Yes. Just let me put my snapper dinner in the fridge. Eating up my profit, don't you know. What's up?"

"I was approached by a man at the grocery store today who seemed interested in learning about my situation. I have no need of interest from another male, as you know. And I have some other concerns that I won't go into just now. I have learned from Mae at the realty office that this fellow is renting the Thomas apartment. Goes by the name of Fairchild—says he's from Colorado. Has he been down to your market? I wondered if you knew anything more about him. Does he strike you as an investigator of some sort?"

"Like DEA, or some such? I guess you might think I would recognize the type. Actually he seems to be a nice ordinary person. Don't know anything about his background, though."

"Oh. Sorry I bothered you during your time with Daniel. I'll be down for some of those grouper fillets in a day or so. Sort of a celebration here."

"Not a problem, Luisa."

The balmy atmosphere and the lazy attitude of the locals led me in natural fashion to procrastinate about another grocery shopping trip and I found myself migrating to the Everglades Rod and Gun Club for another sunset cocktail and dinner. As I entered the screened patio, I found the river scene had been augmented by the presence of a rather large vessel hitched to the pilings in front of the hotel. To me it appeared suitable for open sea sailing. There was a sturdy mast slightly forward with a single heavy sail wrapped tightly around a heavy horizontal structure—I think they call it a boom. There was a spacious cabin above deck with wheel, console, and comfortable salon. The deck and superstructure were dark wood, heavily varnished. The boat appeared to be something close to 40 ft in length.

As I ordered my customary gin on the rocks, I commented to my waitress, "You've added scenery. That's an impressive looking yacht."

"Oh, yes. That's Luisa Alvarez' boat. She sometimes has small groups of visitors out for fishing or sailing. She brought it in early this morning. She lives over in the Plantation section a mile or so east of here. Not enough water there, so she usually anchors it out a ways. But I think there was some problem out there last night." She clearly had no more information to offer and left me with my gin to speculate further.

A few minutes later a pair of very casually dressed fellows, probably in their early forties, drew chairs up at an adjacent table and ordered beers. "I see Luisa has her boat in. She must have clients for a trip."

"Yes, old Manny is there with his dog. He keeps the boat in excellent shape for Luisa."

Drinks were soon delivered by the bar tender, who greeted the men in familiar fashion. "Good to see you. Wouldn't want you to lose touch with the good things in life. I see you haven't decided to go on the wagon."

"Yes, and just the sight of Luisa's beautiful boat provides the atmosphere of the good life. She must have clients again."

The conversation became more intimate and I had to strain to overhear without being obvious.

"Actually, no. There was some trouble last night. Somebody tried to board. Manny shot......" I lost the rest of the conversation. Then, "Luisa went out in the whaler and brought the boat in early this morning to be safe."

My enjoyment of the shrimp scampi was tempered by my curiosity about the event that brought the Glades Lady into the safety of the Barron River.

Next morning I prepared a breakfast of sausage and eggs as I monitored Naples television for any news of maritime activity of an unusual nature. Last evening's TV news did nothing to quench my curiosity and the morning news didn't help. I know I heard the word 'shot'. Had I overheard part of a confidential story that required care in discussion pending disposal of a body?

Although I made an effort to read Marjorie Stoneman Douglas' description of life of the Calusa Indians of southwest Florida, I was unable to ignore the thread of the local marine activity. I donned floppy hat, walking shorts, t-shirt, and Nikes to get a late lunch at Island Seafood. Tourists should be on the wane by now. "Hello Krista. I wonder about those stone crab claws on the menu—is it possible to indulge in a couple of those for my lunch today? I'm not a heavy eater and I'm curious to give them a try—and a beer of course."

"Sorry, the stone crab season just ended. Come back next

fall and we'll crack a couple. You can add some of our mustard sauce and have a go with your fingers."

So back to the conch chowder. I was shortly joined by Krista.

"Pretty special seafood! Right?"

"Yes. But I won't be able to afford those crab claws very often at $4 apiece."

"I know. The tourists and fancy restaurants have discovered them. There is a limited supply. You know, we take just one claw and return the critter to the water. Then we have to wait for him to grow another. Takes a while."

"There was a nice big sailboat at the Rod and Gun Club last evening. I think it was local. Are you familiar with it?"

Krista was gazing down the river, then turned to stare at me briefly. Rather casually she replied, "Yes. The Glades Lady is Luisa Alvarez' boat. She sometimes takes a party of clients out for an outing or a day or two of fishing." Then with a polite smile, "And it's not just a sailboat. The Lady is a motorsailer. She cruises equally well by motor or under sail. And with both she moves out nicely and is quite stable in open water. That's important, especially for a party of guests not used to the open water."

"I know I'm pretty ignorant about such things. I have to believe that you are pretty familiar with boats and such."

She smiled slightly, "You could say that, yes."

This lady could just possibly have made a solo voyage around the world on such a boat! Bears caution and respect.

I decided to do some innocent fishing for information. "I wonder though. That nice a boat must need a lot of care. And might attract some undesirable attention."

She surprised me by continuing with, "All boats require

considerable care. But one like the Glades Lady deserves special attention. Luisa can't afford to keep her tied up by the hotel, so she is anchored out in a sheltered bay that's a bit deeper. Manny Alvarez, I think he's Luisa's uncle, stays on board to care take. In years past, the drug runners targeted boats like that for hijacking. And there are always thieves lurking around to steal the electronics. Boats like that always have a complete array of radios, GPS, and the like."

I added in what I hoped would provoke further comment, "I wouldn't think that would be a problem here, though."

She gave me a thoughtful, slightly suspicious look. Finally she said, "You may be somewhat aware of their trouble last night. Somebody tried to board the Lady. The dog sounded the alarm and Manny fired off a shot in the air from his old Winchester carbine. The intruder jumped overboard and took off in a small boat. The Coast Guard is presently patrolling the area searching for likely suspects. That's why Luisa has the Lady tied up at the hotel."

"I confess I overheard something of that nature. Do you think it was a hijacking attempt?"

"Always a possibility. Probably, though, somebody thought the boat was unattended and an easy mark for the electronics. We have most of that equipment on our boats and have to watch even right here at the dock."

I began to realize this lady wasn't just kitchen help for this little lunch place. "I'm being nosy, and I hope I'm not being offensive. I get the impression that you have a major involvement in this seafood operation."

"Yes, I'm part owner. It's a long story. Maybe some other time."

Krista returned to duties in the kitchen and I gave relaxed attention to the pelicans riding with the tourists on the airboats. After a few minutes of this entertainment, I was distracted by the noisy arrival of an ancient Toyota with small outboard in tow. The driver soon brought his conch chowder to sit at the adjacent table. Upon finishing his chowder, he relaxed to watch the pelicans fishing.

I initiated a sociable comment, "They seem to enjoy diving even if they miss the fish."

"My luck in the Turner River was no better, not like it used to be", was the disgruntled reply of my senior citizen companion. His white-thatched wrinkled visage indicated his experience as a veteran fisherman. He continued, "Been coming here for years. I'm a retired math teacher from Boca; wife gone and kids left the nest. Came to stock up on fish, but just found a few crabs for the pot and a sea cow for company. Guess I will have to shell out for some grouper fillets inside."

"I'm just a very recent visitor. What's the Turner River like?"

"Well, the river crosses the Tamiami Trail a few miles east of here and empties across some oyster reefs into Chokoloskee Bay. I think there used to be a house on the big shell mound a ways back there. I heard a story that when the Park opened, the owner tried to get the government to buy it. They were pretty slow, so he threatened to mine the oyster shells. He had collected enough for a 10 ft mound ready to load onto a barge when they finally coughed up for the property." He laughed, "Tourists probably thought it was a neat Indian shell mound.

I think it's gone now, but the park runs a tour back there occasionally to the historic Indian mound."

I motioned to his vehicle. "Your rig must work pretty well back in the river."

He grumbled, "Sure, but it's no good for open water. Couldn't afford anything bigger on a teacher's salary!"

The weather was moving along towards Florida summer. Morning showers were followed by a buildup of greenish dark clouds with thunder grumbles and jagged lightning in mid-afternoon. The familiarization tour of Everglades City and Chokoloskee didn't take long. No exciting attractions to waste my time, unless I took an interest in snook and redfish. Plenty of days to check things out on foot, but only in early morning or evening. The heat and humidity were legend.

Then I recalled seeing a rack of fat tire bikes on sale at the hardware store. No hesitation there, and I was equipped for all my local travel. And my self-generated breeze evaporated any sweat resulting from pumping the pedals. No problem now in getting lunch and visiting with Krista at the fish market. It was on one of those occasions that I shared a table with a retiree who was well equipped with camera gear. He inquired as to my recommendation of the conch chowder. After a sample from my bowl, he commented, "Not bad at all, although the conch bits are pretty small. Of course I've been spoiled by experiences at Ernie's Bar in Lauderdale. Conch Chowder and Bimini Bread with bite size chunks of conch, walls covered with local contributions of literary graffiti and a fair assortment of used fishing gear. I 'spect it's not there anymore, though."

I continued the conversation with, "Ah, you appear to be an excellent source of local information to keep this traveler from Colorado entertained for a while. Looks like you have been busy with Florida photography too. Get yourself a bowl and join me here; call me Russ."

"Ralph, from Delray on the east coast. I've just been taking advantage of digital equipment to record what's left of Florida wildlife and scenery before it's all gone."

"Well, it all looks pretty spectacular to me. I guess I should make a trip to the National Park. I understand it's one of a kind!"

"It is that! But the wildlife habitat has been badly spoiled by polluted fresh water and saltwater inundation. And the Park facilities have been damaged by hurricanes. About the only improvement I can think of is the fruit stand near the Park entrance. Years ago a young kid had a small table with a sign "Robert is Here!" Now it still has the sign but it's a huge fruit and vegetable market, even including milk shakes with vanilla, chocolate, key lime, or whatever. Picnic tables in the shade too."

We were interrupted by a noisy airboat with megaphone instruction for the tourists to watch for manatee. (Fat chance with all that racket!) Ralph continued, "But if you are looking for the works of a real master, stop at Clyde Butcher's Gallery over on the Trail east of here in the Big Cypress. And take your checkbook. He has images of the real Everglades; not just his large format scenes from the Tamiami Trail, but many that result from wading out in the swamp. And if he is available, you can get an excellent lecture on how we should be taking better care of this environment. I have a suspicion that he has some friends in some rather special nature camps."

"I'll certainly keep that in mind when I'm cruising over that way. Certainly don't plan to do any wading in the swamp on my own."

"I haven't done any of that on my own either, but managed to do the next best thing. A while back I noticed a big old swamp buggy parked by the local bar over near 40-Mile Bend. I stopped in and got myself a beer and struck up a conversation with the rough looking characters who were obviously regulars. Eventually, with a hefty contribution for fuel and tour guide, name of Jasper, I found myself hanging on to my seat for dear life a few inches from the huge tires of that monster swamp buggy as it crashed through the bushes and sawgrass. We flushed a few small flocks of egrets well in advance of our noisy machine and a few alligators avoided the big wheels at the last second. Then as we approached one of the larger tree islands, my scruffy guide gave a nod and questioning look towards a dilapidated shack partly hidden in the palmettos. I nodded and motioned with a free hand towards an open slot in the bushes.

"When he shut off the engine after getting us out onto solid ground he explained, "That's just a shack my buddies and me use when they come out here huntin' deer. It's got a couple of bunks and an old stove that we brought out here for cookin'. You might want to stroll back there through those big m'hogany, though. There's somethin' pretty special back there." I agreed and Jasper led the way along a narrow trail through the bushes. We soon found ourselves in a relatively open area under some very large mahogany trees and several royal palms. Well inside this shelter was a very large native-style chickee, thatched roof and all."

Jasper explained, "Don't guess there's anybody here now, but once in a while a couple pretty impressive dudes come out here in a airboat and have theirselves a party. We could just walk in and look around; best not touch nothin' tho."

There was a pair of comfortable looking single beds, a matching pair of well-used Lazyboys, a standard cook stove and refrigerator connected to small propane tank, and a Formica lunch table with chairs. There were shelves with a scattering of books; I noticed the climate book by Hansen and several by Alex Cook, an unfamiliar author. There was also a stack of CDs, mostly of Kiri te Kanawa; no electronics, they probably brought the necessary with them along with the food and liquor supply. I asked, "Who do you suppose has this setup, and how can they be sure it will be here waiting for them?"

"Well, me and my buddies pick up a little monthly cash donation at the shop back there to be sure this setup stays private. We've never asked for names, but we're pretty sure we know our generous friends. You prob'ly heard the story of the former Florida Judge that kept getting threatened 'cause he was purty generous about throwing the book at crooked politicians   and there was a bunch of 'em. They tried to burn down his house in Palm Beach, so he jest disappeared. And there was a scandal about a state sen'tor that got more than his share of lobby money 'thout doin' a proper job. 'Spect they is purty well fixed to live a quiet life outside the normal s'ciety. We're happy to hep them 'long with whutever!"

Ralph finished his tale with a sly look. "So it's not just the Miccosukee that live back there in the Glades. If you hang about with the not-so-proper folks, you might get introduced to a real interesting part of Florida life!"

I arrived at Island Seafood after most of the tourists had departed. As I sat down with my grouper basket, Ed and Jim, a pair of locals, greeted me. They were discussing a recent conversation with a tourist retired farmer and wife from Nebraska. Apparently they had a friendly discussion about life in Everglades City and experiences in Florida travel. "Farmer Sellon seemed happy to visit. He thought the folks here in town at the hardware store and gas station were pretty friendly. But he had a different feeling for his contacts on the East Coast and down in the Keys. In fact he clearly announced that he would never return there as a tourist and certainly not as a future resident. It seems they got caught in a traffic stop down in Marathon that they felt was an unfair trap. They were moving carefully in heavy double lane traffic when the FHP pulled four drivers over for ignoring a school bus stopped four lanes over on the opposite side of the highway. The busy traffic blocked observations in the vicinity. The cop was careful to explain that the usual rules didn't apply because there was no cement curb around the grassy center divider. No polite warning, just a ticket for $272!! Farmer Sellon insisted on showing us the check stub. Monroe County dropped a thousand bucks in their coffer by pulling over that group of drivers." We agreed that any visits that we might need to make in that area would require exceptional caution and little incentive to engage in local business for gas or meals.

It was a relatively cool, only about 75°, Monday morning.

I had ridden the bike to the store to replenish my milk supply for cereal. As I prepared to depart, the bearded fellow generally known as the recent houseguest of Luisa Alvarez accosted me with, "I've heard someplace that you are that retired university person staying over at the Thomas apartment. I'm John." John's initial appearance and manner suggested that he should be considered a Southwest Florida native, or at least an early settler. The luxurious white beard and well-tended mustache nicely matched the somewhat sparse head of hair. A closer examination indicated a neat modern trim that would not attract attention as a sixties-era hippy. The ponytail was short and well kept, possibly a new addition. John's eyes were a bright and lively green; shallow wrinkles indicated years only slightly beyond middle age.

With my early retirement, I began to feel a kinship. I replied, "Yes, that's correct. I've seen you on the bike occasionally."

"And you were a history professor, right?"

"That's true—didn't know it was common knowledge though."

"Must have heard it someplace. Say, would you like to drop by for a visit sometime?"

"Well, sure. Always good for a visit. Like now, if you can keep my milk cold that is?"

"Just follow me on the bike. Down the road and across the bridge to Luisa's house we go. She's gone down the Trail to stock up on groceries."

The house was a large open structure deep in the mangroves on a small canal. Good ventilation, but with a patio well protected with plastic screen. "We can sit out here with a beer or two in the breeze. The swamp angels that followed us through the mangroves won't venture out in the sun and wind and we're safe behind the screen. At night, though, we have to button up with the A/C to get away from the no-see-ums. They just fly right through the screen. And if we're out for more than a few minutes any exposed skin gets covered with little black specks where they were dissolving our flesh for dinner."

"So I'm being exposed to the real South Florida wilderness. Guess this explains why the population density was never high in the old days." As I watched a Great Blue Heron stalk cautiously along the canal I added, "But it doesn't faze the real natives. That's why visitors like myself come here to see Wild Florida. "

"It's true that the tourists continue to be enthralled by the environment here. And it is truly unique. It is different from anything they are familiar with, in this country or anywhere in the world. The sad thing is that they don't know how marvelous it was in years past. The Everglades and the Big Cypress are dying. The wildlife is disappearing; the habitat is being trashed. Much has been written about it. The famous *River of Grass* and the recent *The Swamp* by Michael Grunwald say it all. Yet no one seems to care, least of all the people who live here now. The experts say, "Florida has lost 90% of its wading birds." We reply, "That's awful; they were special. But they were just birds. The climate is still the best, especially in winter when the bugs are gone."

"Yes, I came to get away from the cold and snow in the long winter in Colorado."

"But you would not have been happy to leave civilization behind to sit out in the sun in the sawgrass or in the swamp here with the snakes and alligators. You expect to have all the comforts of home as well. And so we have modified Nature to suit the hordes of human visitors."

"But the permanent residents here, yourself included, must have the power to control these things. Evidently the development of the trappings of modern human society has priority over the natural habitat."

"Yes, it's the usual story of exploration and exploitation of our land. We find an attractive place and clutter it up with our baggage to make a living. Not just to subsist and enjoy nature, but to dominate and control the land. We have to get rich and powerful, and we do it by attracting tourists and rich retirees to bring the green stuff."

John was well into his second beer and clearly inspired to philosophize about the failings of human society, particularly with regard to his paradise of subtropical Florida. "I under-stand you do some history. I wondered if you might be looking into things about the Calusa. Or just here for the Florida liquid sunshine."

"Mostly the latter, but I might get interested in the Calusa. But I haven't been talking history with anyone and didn't know my professional vita was common knowledge."

"Ah, but it's on the internet, you know. I must confess to doing some Google research. I like to know who my neighbors are these days. And I like to visit with someone about some-thing besides snook. Hope you're not offended."

"No. Not really. Just surprised. So, tell me about yourself. Live here long?'

"Not really. Visited here some and got to know Luisa. We enjoy each other's company so I made a habit of seeing her after her husband died a few years ago."

"But you're not a fisherman."

"Just practicing. I could probably catch enough sheepshead to avoid starving."

Well, not much information about another livelihood or profession. I wonder why. "So, are you knowledgeable about the Calusa?"

"Oh, most folks have heard of the Calusa, but nothing recent of course. Unless you believe Randy Wayne White and his Last Indian. Perhaps you know about the museum of artifacts up at Pine Island. It's probably worth a visit. And you probably ought to take a gander at *Fort Center*; that's a book, author was Bill Sears, a professional archeologist. It's good reading. He announces early on that he had research grants to dig up dead Indians near the big lake. And he gives credit to his local assistants who were illiterate but better workers than his students."

"Maybe later. I'm still getting acquainted with the environment here. You know, identify the birds, and the trees are all different from Colorado too. Tell me though, what are sheepshead"

"Oh, I'm an expert on that. Tell you what, I'll give you a lesson. Say maybe in a week or so, if you have some free time. Oh, here is Luisa with newspapers and stuff from the outside world. I believe you have met."

Luisa was not happy. Before acknowledging my greeting she gave a prolonged stare and frown at John.

John continued, "I've explained to Russ that we discovered that he is a retired history professor. Sounds like a pretty reputable background. Don't you think so Luisa?"

Davie

It was two weeks later that I had guilty thoughts of doing something professional, opened the laptop, and began to search around town for a wireless signal. It was at the coffee house on Chokoloskee that I read the announcement of an Audubon Society workshop on Everglades Restoration at Nova University. My curiosity was aroused and I made plans to attend. It might be good to update my information on *The River of Grass*. And I could make a token inquiry about the present activities of Amy's father, Professor John Orbatz. Might just kill two birds with one stone; drive to the east coast a day early and drop in to see Amy's father.

The trip across I-75 Alligator Alley was a two hour stretch of endless sawgrass and head-to-tail alligators. Certainly unique though: there couldn't be anything like that anyplace else in the world. I arrived at the western sprawl of Ft. Lauderdale in mid-afternoon and checked in at the Audubon-recommended Best Western in Davie. After a rejuvenating cup of coffee at the ubiquitous Starbucks, I began my research of the University. I remembered stories about its infancy with plans to become the 'Harvard of the South'. Rather amusing, considering its initial efforts on an abandoned WWII air base, but it had mushroomed to become the largest independent institute of higher learning in the area. After a prolonged scroll through the lists of various colleges and departments, I found a telephone number for the Office of the Dean of American

Studies. The computerized voice instructed, "If you wish traffic directions to the College of American Studies, punch one now. If you have questions about parking facilities or wish to appeal a parking violation, press two. If you wish details of our curriculum of study, press three. If you wish to obtain counseling about a course of study, press four. If you wish to obtain information on class grades, have your ID and PI available and press five. If you wish to communicate with a member of the faculty and have his or her extension, you may dial that now. If you have other requests, please stay on the line. Have a good day."

Five minutes later, an aggressive female voice said, "Dean's office, this is Madeline. How may I assist you?"

"Ah, good afternoon. I'm calling to arrange an appointment with Professor John Orbatz. Can you arrange that, please?"

"Who is calling, please?"

That sounded ominous, but I promptly replied, "My name is Fairchild. I'm a friend of the family."

"Oh? Could you be more specific?"

"I don't know that we need to get into the family history at this point. His daughter in Colorado suggested that I stop by for a brief chat. I'm sure that Professor Orbatz will understand."

"Professor Orbatz is presently unavailable. If you have her name, I will leave a message for him".

The conversation was puzzling. This was clearly a defensive posture to eliminate unwanted communication with this faculty member. He was unavailable? Such a blunt statement could mean anything from classroom schedule to—who knows?

"This seems to be a somewhat difficult procedure. I'm sure

he knows his daughter's name. I believe I will attempt some more direct method of communication. Thank you. Goodbye!"

Ah, well, no need for such a formal approach. Amy had given me his cell phone number. I should have called that before leaving Everglades City. I asked the Prius to furnish me some air conditioning, then made the call. After listening to a long series of contact attempts, I heard, "Hi. John Orbatz here. I'm not available to take your call just now. Please leave a number and God in Florida will send an angel to look for me. Cheers!" Then a bleep and "The message service for this number is currently unavailable. Sorry". It sounded like the formal standard message that the memory was full. "Come on Orbatz, stop being so hard to get!"

This called for a stop at the 'Lazy Racehorse' and a double Tanqueray on the rocks to quell the frustration. The 'Feedbag' next door beckoned for an early bird dinner. I might as well do that, then retire with feet up to see what earlier generations had seen of John Wayne coping with rustlers and gunslingers. Ah, yes. The New York steak   western beef only—should probably satisfy the gut.

Next morning, after the "Bargain Breakfast" at Denny's, I made a frontal attack on the Department of American Studies. As I waited for recognition in the outer office, I noticed a woman of uncertain age, black hair with streaks of gray and bifocals, at work in a small office at the rear. But I was obviously supposed to be greeted by the blonde at the desk in the front office. This young lady, pert and smiling, was entertaining a pair of casually dressed guys who were obviously hoping to arrange a lunch date with future sexual promise. They hadn't noticed, or were ignoring, the tiny diamond on her left hand. Finally she dismissed their attention and asked, "Can I help you, sir?"

Sounds promising. "Yes, I'm Professor Russell Fairchild, retired from the faculty at Golden West University in Colorado. Could you please direct me to Professor Orbatz' office? I would like to convey my respects and greetings from his family in Colorado."

"Oh, but he's not there—hasn't been for some weeks. Dr. Orbatz is on sabbatical, didn't you know?'

"No, I wasn't aware of that. Is he in town?"

"I'm not sure about that. His activities have been uncertain since the troubles. He has been very secretive about his off campus things since then."

"Troubles? Like what?"

"Some vandalism with his car and apartment. Nothing terribly serious, though. Sorry I can't help you."

"Well, thank you."

What to do? The runaround at the Dean's office began to make sense. Wonder if Amy was aware of these events. I guess I could make a casual call to find out. Then as I ambled out of the office, I noticed that the administrative assistant had left the office before me. She was waiting a short distance down the hall. She nodded at my questioning look.

"Please, let's step into the department reading room here. It's best to be a bit discrete." Then, "I've known Dr. Orbatz for many years and we've shared our problems often. I'm Miriam, American Studies Executive Secretary. I have some concerns about his present situation. It's true that John is officially on sabbatical—you know, scholarly research and all that," said with a slight smirk. "But he has dropped off the planet. I wonder if this is related to the vandalism or perhaps to some personal threats that occurred earlier. He has annoyed a number of influential persons in South Florida with his publications and professional appearances. This may be an independent matter, but just after the last term ended, I received an envelope in the mail with a brief message, the title to his car assigned to me, and an airport parking ticket. His instructions were to take the ticket and retrieve his car and at first opportunity sell it at Car Max. He said to save the signed message in case problems should arise. I'm puzzled and worried about this. I wonder if he is in some kind of trouble".

"It sounds like he may have decided to take a major research trip, or maybe just an extended vacation. But his daughter didn't mention it. I wonder why he is being so secretive."

"I could make some calls and find out his flight destination. There is a fairly narrow time frame that would apply. You know, as if I needed to get his advice on some major financial emergency here. There is a student coffee shop with wireless internet just across the way. Why don't you hang out there while I get busy on this?"

I had worked my way through a pair of slightly stale glazed doughnuts and was about to freshen up my coffee when Miriam reappeared. She was excited. "Pay dirt on the third call. He had reservations on Frontier to Denver at 2 that day." But then, with a worried look, "He checked in, but didn't board. Something must have happened."

"Well, he's probably not in Denver. But it's hardly likely that he ran into some foul play at the airport."

"And if he's in a local hospital, we would surely have heard by now. I guess I should check anyway."

"I'll leave that to you. I'm sure you'll be much more efficient. Do you have his home address? I'll go there. If he returned there for some reason, there should be some indication."

"Oh my! If he collapsed or something, no one would know. I'll get the address. Give me your cell number and I'll get back to you in a few minutes."

Orbatz' apartment was only a few blocks away. All was quiet—no response to doorbell or knocking. As I considered the possible next steps, the apartment manager appeared. "Ain't nobody there. Lease expired. I'm cleaning for a new rental next month."

"I was looking for Dr. John Orbatz. Do you know his whereabouts now?"

"Nope. Left a couple months ago. The lease was paid up till last week."

Another dead end. Might as well do the Audubon Workshop thing so as not a complete waste of trip. I discovered I had missed an introductory session; the second session had to do with funding matters—pretty disillusioning. My cell phone buzzed half way through and I left to get the report from Miriam.

"Professor Fairchild, I inquired at the four nearest hospitals for our missing professor. Not there—never was! I'm at a complete loss."

"I see what you mean. His daughter didn't mention any of this. In retrospect, she made a rather pointed effort to get me to look him up. She seemed overly casual, but I'll see if she has some explanation or clue we don't know about."

That effort produced more frustration: contact with a machine and a request to leave a number. I stopped at the nearest fast food—don't remember what I ate. With brain swirling with new confusion, I had no inspiration to sit through a tedious workshop. I settled in to the last dependable resort, the Prius, and headed back to Everglades City.

The sun was beginning to add a few calories to the 85% humidity as I cruised along a side street towards my abode. About midway on the journey my cell phone gave a jingle. It was the return call from Amy.

"Dr. Fairchild, I got your call and brief message. I take it that you visited Nova University. I wondered if you were able to see Dad."

"Hi Amy. Yes and No. Your father seems to be leading a rather mysterious life. He's on sabbatical, but his whereabouts is uncertain. I just thought I should report my effort to you."

"Oh dear. I am sorry for your trouble. In fact, we've been out of touch with him for a month or so. That isn't too unusual, but now I wonder. Should I be worried?"

"Well, I checked his office and apartment, which didn't reveal any obvious problems. But I discovered he had a ticket to Denver on Frontier, but was a no show. Were you aware of his plans, perhaps to visit you?"

"Oh, my no! Look, I will be visiting Mother in a week or so, hopefully before hurricane season. They are divorced, but we can probably figure something out. Sorry for your trouble, though. I didn't mean for you to spend your time being a private detective. We should reimburse you for the trip expense. We'll have you over for a dinner and a movie or something."

"Oh, I won't refuse such offers, but it's not necessary for

this slight effort. Keep in touch, though. I'm curious about this situation."

"Well, thanks again for your trouble. Please don't give it another thought. And enjoy that Florida sunshine."

"I certainly will. Goodbye." So, nothing in that conversation to clarify matters. But I won't stop wondering.

It was just a week later that I was gradually brought back to reality from my brief Sunday afternoon nap by a persistent summons from my cell phone. Then the hot and humid Florida atmosphere contributed to my inefficient searching and clumsy groping and I missed the call. But I noted the 954 area code for Ft. Lauderdale. Perhaps there would be news about Amy's father. I punched the icon to return the call.

"Hello, this is Amy."

"Oh, Amy. Russell here, returning your call that I just missed."

"Yes Prof. Surprise! I'm here in Florida at Mother's house with family. Remember I mentioned that possibility the last time we talked. I thought I would touch bases with you. Enjoying the warm sunshine, are you?"

"Of course. Actually beginning to relax like a native."

"Good. Now, the reason I'm calling is to say that Albert and I are planning a trip to your neck of the woods—or maybe I should say the swamp—on Friday. My son is going to stay with Mother. We're going to visit the Audubon Corkscrew Swamp Sanctuary north of you and expect to come down to Everglades City for dinner before driving back here. I thought we might have a short visit with you over dinner."

"Sounds great! I recommend the Everglades Rod and Gun Club. Meet you there—say when."

"Oh, say about 6, give or take a few minutes. I guess we can find it in that big city."

"Not a problem! See you there. Enjoy the swamp and its critters."

I was debating about ordering my second Tanqueray when Albert and Amy arrived on the patio. Amy greeted me with, "Oh, my! This is a neat place. Looks like you've settled in like a decrepit snowbird. We'll join you for margaritas when you freshen up your whatever. I doubt you're drinking Everglades water!"

With delivery of the drink order, Amy began a glowing description of Corkscrew. "The Audubon Society has done a spectacular job of developing the swamp into a first class tourist destination. They have built a 2-mile boardwalk through the bald cypress swamp with a variety of shelters to escape rain showers or just sit quietly to watch and listen to birds and other swamp critters. A leisurely walk can take several hours. And the entrance facility is relatively new with beautiful exhibits, a modest tea room, and a well stocked gift shop, of course."

Amy continued her explanation. "The Audubon literature described their management of that 45 square kilometers of swampland as a wildlife sanctuary 50 some years ago. It was one of the last sections of bald cypress timber that had escaped logging. There are lots of patches of pond cypress in South Florida; they are small trees and not much good for timber. But bald cypress can be something like 6 feet in diameter and

70 feet tall. I'm not sure why they call them bald, though—maybe because they lose their needles in the fall. They grow in the swamp with these knees sticking up from the roots; I guess they furnish air to the roots or something. The volunteer guides explained that those trees used to be prime nesting habitat for wood storks. It is past nesting season, of course, but we were told that they didn't nest this year. The birds only nest when the water level is good: too much water and they can't find the fish or whatever, and if it is dry, there's no food. We didn't see any storks in the swamp, but there were a few circling around way up high. They call the storks an indicator species because they react to the habitat. And now they are an endangered species because of poor habitat—water levels and water quality for their food."

Amy added, "It was a spectacular place, but disappointing because the birds were gone. It was awfully quiet."

I replied, "You know, I've read something of the Audubon Society's efforts to preserve that habitat. They saved that section of bald cypress and made it available to visitors. It must have been an exciting place when the wood storks were making good use of that nesting habitat. But then developers began a drainage project for a huge subdivision to the south that is threatening the water supply. I guess I'll have to visit soon and try to imagine how it must have been."

We were well satisfied with dinner and were patiently awaiting coffee when Amy finally mentioned the subject of her father. "You know, we didn't communicate often with Dad after the divorce, just assumed he was getting along OK. He had a good established position at Nova with no financial problems and good health. Now Mother tells us that there have been rumors that he has been subjected to some nasty threats and even attacks like arson and sabotage to his car. And you've found that he hasn't been seen or heard from for several months. We worry about foul play, but there's no evidence of that. He just seems to have disappeared. We appreciate your checking into the situation at Davie. Have you learned anything since then?"

"No. There wasn't much to follow up on. Do you have any new leads?"

"Not really. We are continuing to visit with friends of the family and people at the university, but nothing helpful has turned up. We don't want to impose on your relaxation time here but we would be grateful if you could continue to keep the situation in mind. And we've brought pictures that might be useful." Amy signaled a pause with a hand wave and rummaged in her purse. "Here is a picture of Dad with Mother and I taken a few years ago. And this one arrived with a Christmas card a year or so ago. It appears it was taken on a boat with some friends   might have been a fishing trip. I thought someone in this fishing town might make some sense of it."

The family picture was a fairly formal affair with Mrs. Orbatz and Amy slightly to the rear and flanking Professor Orbatz. He was of medium height and average build, with iron gray hair, dressed in a suit and tie, casually holding his glasses at rest. Amy had a huge smile, and mother and father both had pleasant expressions. This was clearly a young healthy family. The boating picture was of a group of six casually dressed men, probably aged late forties or early fifties. All were wearing short-sleeved sport shirts with open neck and long trousers of various shades of blue or brown. The pictures made me more optimistic that I could find someone who recognized the professor. At least I now knew his appearance. And I was becoming increasingly curious about the Orbatz history. "You know, I'm aware that most Florida residents are from the Northeast or maybe the Midwest, very few really native. What is the origin of the Orbatz name?"

Amy began an explanation, "It is rather unusual. In one of the earlier generations of tourists there was a visitor from Eastern Europe, named Orbatz. In one of his Everglades tours, he crossed paths with a Seminole family. There was a dark haired maiden whom he found attractive and he wooed her with gifts and the promise of high society. She was excited to leave the Glades with him and become his native princess. Eventually there was a son who was uniquely endowed to lead the Seminoles to a comfortable status with the northern settlers. He was my grandfather. He married a social butterfly from Palm Beach and they sent their son John off to become a Yale graduate. He returned to Nova University with my mother from Massachusetts." Amy paused, "It was never a quiet marriage. Mother has never appreciated why he would occasionally go off into the Glades to visit with the Miccosukees."

At lunch the following day, I showed the pictures to Krista. "There's a family from my university in Colorado that has been searching for the woman's father. He was a faculty member at Nova University near Ft. Lauderdale and he is missing under mysterious circumstances. There's some concern about foul play but no evidence that justifies asking the authorities for help. His daughter has asked me as a favor to give some thought to the situation, ask around where he might have visited. I thought these pictures might be useful. One's a family photo; the other is some kind of outing."

Krista placed her chowder carefully on the table and accepted the pictures. "The gentleman in the family photo looks familiar somehow, could have been one of the tourists. That covers lots of territory though so it doesn't help much. And yes, the other looks very much like a fishing trip. They are grouped together on a boat of some kind; the man in question is holding a fishing lure, a plug for snook, I would guess. That would certainly be appropriate for this area. Why don't you ask Luisa if she is familiar with the group, or might be able to suggest other fishing guides to talk to? If he's been fishing in this area, he'll be back!"

"Oooh, she'll probably think this is an outlandish way for me to start a conversation with her!"

"I see her occasionally. I told her you're a good customer and a gentleman—and you'll find the jar for tips inside."

The pictures were getting a bit worn from nesting in my shirt pocket for a week before I crossed paths with Luisa and John at the laundry. "Hello again. Krista may have mentioned to you that I might be asking you for information. I'd like your advice about these pictures given to me by the lady in this family photo. She has asked me for help in searching for her father; he's the family man in the picture. And we think the other is a group of fishermen with her father on the right. Thought you might have crossed paths with them on some occasion or could suggest other guides to ask. We suspect they may have been on an outing in this area; if so, he might return some time. What do you think?"

Luisa took a glance at the fishing group and started a quick smile. Pay dirt? But the smile disappeared and she stood at rigid attention staring at the photo. Then, carefully shifting her eyes to the family photo, she appeared lost in thought. "Interesting photos, yes. I wish I could help you; you better look at these, John."

With that remark, she moved very purposefully to stand facing John; she was in such a position that I was unable to see her expression. John stared at her for long seconds with his head slightly cocked. He accepted the pictures, then turned away abruptly, presumably to get better light to examine the photos. His delay in reply suggested to me that the photos required some special examination. But when he turned to hand me the pictures, he seemed to find some humor in the situation. He said only, "Remarkable photos. You may need some luck in your search though. I will be very interested in your results. Keep in touch, won't you?"

In retrospect, I made a fateful decision in the next days. Assuming that Luisa and John had given me a definitive decision about any visitation by Amy's father, I neglected to contact any of the other local guides. In the future days and weeks I visited a number of fishing guides and charter facilities in Goodland and Marco, but with no success.

As I paid for breakfast at the Ivey House the next week, I noted the opportunity to join an evening kayak tour to an egret rookery. That sounded like a chance to get an intimate exposure to Everglades birdlife. I asked, "Will this business with a paddle be too much for a Colorado mountain man? Do you guarantee 911 service out there?"

Bertha laughed and replied, "Our guides have yet to call for helicopter rescue. And we haven't lost anyone out there recently. Or at least they never returned to complain. Of course, the alligators do a thorough job of cleaning up." This apparently was her idea of a joke, but my worried look caused a change to serious. "Really, it's a pleasant trip. It's a good idea to take mosquito repellent though."

"OK, just add the fee to my breakfast tab and I'll check in with the guide this afternoon for survival instructions."

We were blessed with an unusually quiet late afternoon, a few fair weather cumulus and no precip. Our group was treated like royalty, with the guide manhandling the equipment while we gazed doubtfully at each other. "Paddle, life preserver, and headlamp, wade a few steps to your kayak and we're off. The life preserver is just to look official. If you capsize, remember to stand vertical; the water is all of a foot deep!"

I had no difficulty using the paddle to accomplish some motion, but persuading the kayak to follow the guide was more of a challenge. He was patient, however, and we were soon strung out in a convoy of about a hundred yards. I brought up the rear: someone must protect our group from hungry alligators, don't you know.

An hour's sweat and baby blisters brought our group to a small island of mangroves decorated with splashes of something white. The egrets had evidently visited at some time in the past, but were not now present. The guide advised, "We'll take a breather here and watch the sunset. I have the birds scheduled to arrive just as the sun touches the horizon."

I was ready for the breather and sure enough, three egrets arrived on schedule. They perched in the outermost branches of the mangroves to permit themselves a good view of the tourists. Shortly afterward, a dozen or so stragglers joined the flock. The sun disappeared and it was suddenly dark. The show was over.

Someplace in the gloom came the instruction, "Headlamps on. Follow me!"

The stars were not yet bright enough in the twilight to do celestial navigation so I diligently followed the little red light on the back of the guide's head. Fortunately, the guide stopped paddling every five minutes to do a kayak count. Finally, back at the launch site, we were welcomed by swarms of mosquitoes and the tour was concluded.

I recounted our experience to Krista at lunch the next day. "That rookery was something less than spectacular. I rather expected a thousand or so noisy egrets jostling each other for a roosting site. This was a rather sorry example of Everglades birdlife. I thought to ask for my money back, but the guide had no apology. He said, "That's just the way it is now!"

Krista sympathized with my disappointment. "Your guide was correct, but should have explained the situation in advance. Of course, he probably would have lost most of his customers. You see, Florida has lost 90% of its wading birds. The developers and agriculture, especially Big Sugar, have fouled up the water situation. The water quality is no longer suitable for making food for the birds and the water levels don't vary with the proper timing to give the nesting birds a chance to feed their young: if it's dry, there isn't any food and if the water is too deep, the birds can't catch anything. Most tourists think the Everglades scenery is unique and beautiful, but they don't realize that the wildlife is almost gone."

"I suppose this area is downstream of the pollution sources and that is bad. And it must affect the fishing too, doesn't it? Is there any way to repair the situation?"

"You're correct. The fish nurseries have been badly damaged. Florida Bay is a desert of polluted water. This area is a little better, but the fishing pressure is a problem. We try to conserve, but have to work hard just to break even on expenses. Some of our competitors have thrown in the towel and have gone to work building houses for the snowbirds and tourists like you."

"Ouch!" I began to understand why Krista had a less than cordial attitude towards me and the other customers. We were a necessary evil! "Well, I will continue to buy your shrimp basket and conch chowder. And the construction workers at least have jobs. And the developers are still making money on those ugly condos!"

Krista's glance toward me at this point was slightly apologetic. We were in this together.

Krista was absent the following day at lunchtime. I learned that she was filling in for a crewmember on one of the boats; he was out with the flu. That would explain how she managed to stay so trim and husky. A thought: if I hoped to make a positive impression on this lady, I ought to convert some of the flab around my waist and the drooping flesh under my arms into useful muscle. Krista had not shown any sign of potential interest, but perhaps some attention to my general appearance would be a generally positive move. Perhaps some improvement there would partially compensate for some fifteen years age difference. Then again, maybe not.

Everglades City had not yet succumbed to a need for a workout gym with weights and fancy machines, but I had once felt some pride in sit-ups, push-ups, and chinning activities. Time to reactivate those muscles. And long walks in the evening and early mornings would be good, maybe some fast moves to get the circulation going again. I needed a goal though. Ah! A hundred sit-ups, fifty push-ups, and twenty chin-ups and I would be ready. Then I would bravely approach Krista for a dinner date, evening movie, whatever. Clearly I was reverting to teenage behavior. Nothing ventured, nothing gained. I would ignore the thought of "no fool like an old fool!"

A few days later, in early morning, I decided to augment my push-ups with a bike ride out to Chokoloskee. As I circled past the tennis courts downtown, I saw John and Luisa engaged in a leisurely game of tennis. I gave them a wave and thought I might stop on my return for a brief visit, assuming they would be ready for a breather. After stopping at the coffee shop on Chokoloskee, I realized I had delayed too long for my projected conversation. But as I approached the turnoff to Plantation Key I saw the Everglades City Marshall's vehicle departing. This was an unusual patrol in midday, so I wheeled down the street to see what might have happened. There were several cars parked near the entrance to Luisa and John's place, so I proceeded to be nosy and investigate. At the house, concerned neighbors surrounded Luisa and John and I learned that there had been a robbery. An excited and very talkative lady informed me that a small boat was beating a hasty retreat down the canal when my friends returned from tennis. But most of an hour had passed before they realized that the house had been entered.

Making myself known to John, I offered my condolences. "Sorry to hear about the break-in. I would think that is unusual here; the perps must have known you were at the tennis courts. Did you lose valuables?"

"Only a little. They ignored Luisa's jewelry, but got my laptop. That's a nuisance, but we had backup for important data like house insurance and boat records."

Luisa added, "John uses the computer to work on his book about the Florida environment, but that's backed up on CD too."

"Maybe the thief wanted your manuscript to get your secrets about water pollution, or maybe just to beat you to publication."

With some hesitation John replied, "Yes, I have to wonder. That information would be an eye opener to certain individuals. It's worrisome to think Big Sugar or the developer of a particular big condo project had any idea that I might be working to expose their activities. That had crossed my mind though, and I took precautions to keep it safe. It wasn't on computer, only on the backup disc."

Luisa interjected, "Oh, John! Do you suppose...?"

The conversation ended abruptly. I took the hint and prepared to depart. "If I can be of use to help you replace the laptop, let me know."

Thinking about going to the Corkscrew Sanctuary, I

decided to check for Orbatz publications. Of the several on the topics of Florida birds, there was one whose title clearly identified Big Sugar as a major contributor to Everglades water degradation with phosphate fertilizer. Now there was a potential troublemaker who might have caused Orbatz' disappearance in some fashion, either directly or at least by threat.

I would at least follow up on my moral obligation to Amy with a visit to Audubon Corkscrew. She had indicated that it was a major tourist attraction for naturalists, so her father would undoubtedly have visited there too. Perhaps there would be some recent contact of a personal nature that would give me a clue to his present whereabouts and activities.

After a leisurely breakfast I pointed the Prius northward up the straight-shot two-lane blacktop. It was a standard hot sultry Florida day, with little threat of thunderstorms. The mangroves gradually merged into a jungle of nondescript trees along the canal. An occasional alligator or black eagle-—some had red heads—relieved the boredom somewhat. And there was a large white bird with long black bill standing on one leg every hundred yards or so. My sudden arrival in Immokalee was a culture shock. This was Florida farm country, with tomatoes, cows, and the southern fringe of orange groves. On the outskirts I passed a neat subdivision of very modest but neat houses that just might be the outgrowth of Bobby Kennedy's visit many years ago. After a few warehouses with lots of tomatoes and a farm implement dealer with acres of huge tractors, I found myself at a major intersection in the town center with a McDonald's and a prominent sign for Corkscrew.

After passing the new Seminole casino on the edge of town, there were few other indications of human habitation until my arrival at Corkscrew. The supermarket size parking lot was almost full! I had betrayed my novice bird watching status by arriving in late morning. The lobby of the visitor center reminded visitors of the Audubon connection with an overwhelming display of Audubon prints. A uniformed volunteer was delighted to accept my entrance fee and point me to the gift shop for further potential extraction of cash. I wandered through the forest of binoculars and t-shirts featuring storks until I found a blue-haired lady with bifocals who appeared ready for a nice visit. "Good morning. Welcome to Corkscrew, and may I be of some help?"

"Well, I plan to find my way to the boardwalk eventually, but I have a personal problem to take care of first."

"The Men's Room is there in the lobby just to your left."

"Ah, yes. But later." Then extracting the wrinkled pictures of Orbatz, I explained. "You see, I have a friend in Colorado who has asked me to search for her father. Since he was a naturalist of sorts, we suspect he might have visited here, perhaps recently."

"Oh my, I'm just a volunteer and only here one day a week." With a quick glance at the pictures, she added, "Emily is regular staff; she's here in the office. Let's check with her."

Emily was obviously surprised and disappointed to be asked a question unrelated to the refuge, but she dutifully examined the photos. I explained, "I'm searching for Professor Orbatz of Nova University at the request of his daughter in Colorado. He is the man in the center in the family picture and on the right in the photo which appears to be some sort of outdoor outing, perhaps a fishing tour."

Emily raised eyebrows and surprised me with, "Oh yes, we

know him well. He has consulted with us frequently about the refuge and we have one of his books here in the gift shop. In fact, he did a book signing with us last year. But I haven't seen him recently. I take it you are having some difficulty in catching up with him. He does move about quite a bit."

"Yes, I understand that he is on sabbatical, but his departure from the university was a bit mysterious and his daughter is concerned. I had hoped you might be able to give us a lead on where to search."

"Well, assuming he continues to be actively involved with environmental things, you might check with National Audubon. He might be doing some consulting or research with them. I am aware that he is somewhat controversial with much of the commercial establishment and he has asked us to be discrete with information. You are clearly not a threat, but you will probably have to visit National up in Maitland in person to secure any information on his whereabouts. I wish you luck. And I hope he's not in any difficulty; he's been a good friend of the environment and we've enjoyed his visits."

I visited the Men's Room and made my way to the boardwalk. The professor was not quite so mysterious and I was in mutually friendly territory. But the element of threat was more real. A drive to Maitland was a duty to Amy that did not greatly appeal to me. I would have to give it some thought sometime in the future. For now the boardwalk and its remnant forest of bald cypress would be my indirect communication with the elusive professor. I found a bench sheltered from the sun and the threat of a shower from a grumbling small dark cloud. There was a distant birdcall; I was fairly certain it was not my friendly Midwestern robin. It was otherwise quiet. No breeze disturbed the monstrous leaves in the foreground as if the swamp were taking a noontime nap. But there was no water in the swamp! My tourist companions who moved past were similarly perplexed with this dry swamp. We finally arrived at a muddy pond where a small wading bird with yellow feet was attempting to stir up some lunch from the shallows.

I crossed paths with John at the hardware store a few days after my Corkscrew visit. He reminded me that I was due for a fishing lesson. "I don't think I can get Luisa to crank up the Lady for you, but I could get you started in the canal. Why don't you come by some early evening, maybe tomorrow, about 5? We can sit on the dock with a beer and wet a line. Snook would be pretty doubtful, but we might attract some mangrove snappers. And bring mosquito repellent."

I pedaled the fat tire bike down Plantation Parkway to John's house about 4:30 the next afternoon. There had been a morning shower and there was a very large cumulonimbus with a menacing greenish-violet base to the north, but it appeared to be grumbling its way eastward. I interrupted John at his computer. "Well now, that line of thought wasn't going anywhere anyway. Catching some panfish will be at least as productive and a lot more fun. Spare rod for you there by the door; I'll get bait from the freezer. The chairs are on the dock waiting for us. Luisa is patching some of my old jeans—best not to disturb her!"

The business part of my tackle consisted of a nylon line on a little rod with a white bobber and a small chunk of lead attached, ending in a small hook. John speared half a frozen shrimp on the hook and said, "You take it from here; just drop that over the end of the dock and hang on to the rod. Best drink your beer now. You'll be too busy in a few minutes."

It was a short minute before the bobber showed signs of life and in another 10 seconds it disappeared into the murky depths and I felt a sharp tug as the tip of my little fishing rod dipped toward the water. My lesson on the reel gadget had been very brief and I quickly had the nylon line free and streaming into the creek.

"No! Don't touch it—you'll slice your hand. Here, just turn that crank."

So I retrieved a lot of loose line until it came up solid. I had the rod tip at 45° looking towards the far shore, but that was it. "Ah a big one! What do I do now?"

"Ah, the little rascal has you hooked on the mangrove roots over there." John tapped my shoulder, "Sorry, should have warned you. Let's see if I can rescue your tackle—we may have to break the line." John gave the line a few sharp jerks and then said, "Step away from the line—it may snap back at us." He cranked up all the slack line and then backed slowly away. The line must have stretched a foot or so and then grudgingly came free with about three feet of mangrove root. "OK, back to square one. Bait up and catch the little monster this time!"

So after releasing my initial catch, I carefully added a new morsel of shrimp and cast—actually just dropped—the bait into the canal. Almost immediately the bobber gave signs of a nibble. John warned, "He's about to bite; be ready." As I glanced at John, the bobber disappeared and there was a vicious tug on the line. "Hey! A strike!" (Isn't that what it's called?)

John spoke up, " Quick! Reel him in before he gets to the mangroves!"

The tip of my rod was seesawing up and down from the turmoil and splashing at the end of the line as I diligently cranked in my prize. "Must be about 10 pounds, suppose?" John grinned. My 6-inch fish was not about to give up as I lifted him up to the dock. John warned, "Watch that top fin as you unhook him. Then drop him in that pail of water; there's another one waiting for you out there."

"But he's just a baby; shouldn't I put him back to grow some more?"

"He's as ready for the frying pan as he'll ever be. Now let's see who can get us to an even dozen first."

In slightly less than an hour we were exhibiting our catch to Luisa. "Don't look at me to clean them. But I suppose if you scale and gut them and marinate them in some rum for 30 minutes, they might go good with some pole beans and spinach."

And so they did! So ended my first fishing expedition.

A week later I pedaled the bike to the hardware store on Collier Ave. to shop for fishing gear. I thought to duplicate the spinning reel and light tackle that John had loaned me. But I found there was a variety of impressive fishing gear that might make me look like a serious sportsman. I tried the heft of one of the stubby rods with 6-inch reel and heavy line. It was clearly meant for a contest with a pick-on-someone-your-own-size creature—perhaps suitable for swordfish? A voice near my elbow suggested, "Ah, looks like you're looking to equip your 24 ft Mako for a trip out to the Gulf. They tell me that the redfish are a very respectable size out there—if you know the right spots. I'm Charley, and that outfit, along with bait bucket, gaff, or landing net, goes for about $250."

"Oh, but that's a little steep for my budget. And I don't even have a boat. How about something suitable for whatever might be lurking a few feet from shore?"

"You'll have to forgive me. I was just kidding about what you might be dreaming. Seriously though, if you wander on up to Cap's, he could arrange for a guided trip out to the big time. Comes with all the gear and a promise to find fish. Actually, I think he has a few spots charged with chum—he drives right out to the GPS site."

"Still a dream I'm afraid. I wonder though. Does Luisa do that sort of thing—I see her boat is tied up at the hotel."

"No, not her cup of tea. And they brought the boat in close while they are out of town. Luisa said they're making a personal visit, flew to Chicago out of Lauderdale on Frontier." Charley beckoned me to the next aisle for tackle my size. "I believe I would recommend that you hang out over on the Barron River or out on the causeway across the bay to Chokoloskee. I could fix you up with a cast net for pinfish bait. Or get yourself charged up with frozen shrimp or cut mullet for bait; or get a little exercise with a plug or lure for maybe a snook. And there's plenty of casting room for a beach rod; gives you more range. You might even want to take it over to the Gulf sometime."

So I ended up with maybe more gear than my bike could handle.

A few days later, I was ready for some not very serious

conversation with Krista about my introduction to fishing as a retirement pastime, but she seemed to be missing. I learned that she had departed to make bail for one of her boat crew who was in the slammer after getting down to his skivvies on top of the tourist tower on the way to Chokoloskee. Some story about getting a little silly after indulging in a combination of Jack Daniels and marijuana."

I had learned to make a morning check with Dell on the internet for the Naples News website for local happenings. I gave careful attention to the fishing forecast—but it didn't mention the Everglades City waters. I don't usually bother to check e-mail; my fan club is quite small. But there it was—a note from Amy at Golden West.

To: Russell
From: Amy

Hello, Prof. You must be getting a good tan and putting on weight with Florida lobsters. Good!!! Just a note to bring you up to date about my Dad. No need for you to continue a search. He showed up here the other day with his new companion. Looking good, no problems. Except they are still being careful about exposure to mischief from some of Prof's students, Big Sugar, or whatever.

Cheers
Amy

Ah so! That project solved. But I'm still curious about Orbatz' whereabouts here in Florida.

I was standing with a beer on the dock at the Island Market, scanning the tidal flow for a manatee when John with the whiskers, just returned from Chicago, appeared in my line of sight. "Ah, the professor is enjoying his retirement in my front yard. But the snow has all melted in Colorado and the trees have new leaves; you're missing all the seasons that we don't have here!"

"Hello John, Luisa must have you shopping for fresh grouper. Yes, that's another world! But I overheard a remark at the hardware store that you had made a trip up that way. Must have been a special occasion!"

John stared at me with a resigned smile. "Yes, a somewhat neglected family matter that was brought to my attention by your arrival. Your search for Orbatz at the request of a caring family member at your college made me realize my selfish concerns with personal pleasure and safe disposition. I trust that you may sympathize with this situation where there have been, and continue to be, some circumstances that suggest caution for the physical safety of our Professor Orbatz. I trust that my relationship with you may continue with this in mind."

I now view that as what could be called a pregnant pause. Obviously, John's comments were directly related to my earlier search for Orbatz. I had been relaxed by Amy's note of his visit to the West; I had given little further thought of his whereabouts. Was this a request for continued close friendship with an apology for a previous deception? Or was this simply a confession of personal guilt in a similar situation? Was the reference to physical safety related to Amy's expression of "exposure to mischief"? I stared with open mouth at John's apologetic expression.

Was John's casual friendship simply recognition of our positions as caring intellectuals thrown together in the troubled environment of South Florida? Or was it possible that this bearded one was actually a mellowed version of the professorial John Orbatz of Nova University? The possibilities were almost, but not quite, believable. And I was not about to admit to my naïveté.

I nodded with a chuckle. "I'll spring for a couple of beers if you'll join me."

"Don't mind if I do. We can sit here and be content with our spot in paradise. Our slight difficulties here are nothing compared with the rest of the world."

The Greenwich Lady

I was nursing a glass of pinot noir while preparing some frozen peas for the microwave. The baked grouper had about 7 minutes to go for dinner. The TV was on Channel 4 News, mostly to keep me company with background chatter. I heard, "We have breaking news. We have received a video of the Greenwich couple that was abducted from their sailboat on May 28. Our interpreter is here with their message."

"They state that their names are Jay and Abby Whitmore. They were holding last evening's edition of El Espectador, Bogotá's newspaper, and ask that friends and relatives in Connecticut take their attendant's demand for ransom seriously. Abby says, "We've been treated well, but our captors are becoming impatient." Jay interrupted, "We've just been told to not say any more."

Announcer, "I believe this is the first communication from the Connecticut couple since they were abducted from their boat. The Coast Guard has released this photo of the motorsailer at the scene in the Florida Straits. You will recall that the US Coast Guard was notified of an abandoned motorsailer near Cozumel. When boarded, the crew discovered a ransom note for One Million Dollars attached to the wheel. The vessel had been thoroughly ransacked, including ripped-out wall panels below deck. However, none of the expensive electronics was disturbed. The FBI and DEA are not discussing the situation beyond notifying families in Connecticut and U.S. embassies in the Caribbean."

The peas were patiently awaiting my attention after a 2 minute zap. They were being ignored in favor of the pinot noir, and I had developed an increased interest in the plight of the Connecticut couple. It was the photograph of the motorsailer being towed by the Coast Guard Cutter that drew my attention. As the news helicopter circled the stern of the motorsailer, I got a brief glimpse of the part of the name: I saw "Lady", and that brought a vision of the Glades Lady in trouble. Closer inspection revealed Greenwich Lady, but I was now giving the story my full attention. The situation was of some more intimate concern.

The story continued, "In a possibly related matter, you may recall that the DEA announced a major drug bust in Miami a few weeks ago. In response to an anonymous tip, they found over 3 million in street value cocaine in an abandoned warehouse in south Miami. Our reporter on the scene at this boat suggests it looks like a drug transaction gone sour. The Whitmore couple was well established in social circles at the yacht club in Greenwich and they own an attractive 5-bedroom house near the waterfront. They were evidently just returning from a 4-month sailing trip to the Mediterranean. We have no information on family efforts to organize assets for purpose of the ransom."

My excitement had cooled considerably as the news story switched to the huge new contract for the Dolphin's quarterback and I engaged the mute button to enjoy my fish dinner.

There was a simultaneous conversation taking place in a completely different universe. Peter Wallace had just finished being debriefed by his boss in the Washington DEA office. "So our information on the drug shipment from Colombia worked well for the raid in Miami, but we missed the cash transfer somehow. Now we suspect it went back to Cozumel with that motorsailer, but the boat is missing from the Yucatan marina."

In his nondescript office on Massachusetts Avenue, Max nodded and propped his Florsheims on the corner of the desk. "Yes, we did well to take those drugs out of circulation. And your undercover work on that raid at Everglades City a while back put an end to that silly smuggle operation of Square Grouper. We had to put a few away for a short stay, but generally it gave the locals a necessary lesson. Sorry to have kept you in the slammer overnight, but we've spread the rumor that you escaped in transfer."

Max continued unhappily. "But now we need to recover that cash or they will use it to finance other transfers. I understand your undercover status is still solid. Why don't you mosey down there and investigate the situation with that boat? Catch a night flight to Miami—sorry about your evening plans at Kennedy Center. You have authority to set up any action you believe appropriate—let us know in the usual way. Oh, and I'm sure your expense voucher went through this morning. The check will be deposited in the same manner as the monthly pay."

A few days later, I had just switched the TV to Channel 4 before retiring, thinking to get a weather forecast for the next day—probably something like " brief shower in early AM, noontime temperature in mid 80's, followed by PM thunderstorm, clearing in the evening". But I heard, "This just in: The kidnapped Connecticut couple missing in the Caribbean are safe. Our investigating correspondent forwarded this message from Jay Whitmore:

"Our Colombian caretakers have decided that we were getting to be a social nuisance, so they announced that we were going for a ride. It sounded ominous, but they just put us in their launch and dumped us in a big inflatable with bottles of water someplace in the Caribbean. And then they gave the US Coast Guard our GPS coordinates and we were picked up in a matter of hours. I guess they must have figured there would be less heat on their friends in that Miami raid if they turned us loose. And the Lady was fully insured, so we've been very lucky."

The commentator added, "The DEA office in Miami had no comment."

The Glades Lady

I spotted John's bike propped against the cabbage palm at the Post Office. I pretended a need to check my vacant box, "John, are you familiar with that motorsailer abandoned and adrift in the Florida Straits south of the coast here? The pictures on TV looked exactly like Luisa's boat."

"We never watch TV—we get our news on the internet. Didn't see that video though."

"I thought it looked awfully familiar. When I saw the name on the stern, I got a glimpse of "Lady"—made me give it my full attention. But it turned out to be the Greenwich Lady from Connecticut."

"Name sounds a bit familiar; we might have crossed paths someplace. Let's get Luisa to pull up a copy and see if it is another motorsailer. Then see if she remembers it."

So John carefully stacked an Audubon magazine and some junk mail in a plastic bag; it proclaimed 40 years of grocery service to Everglades City. I sorted through an even dozen requests for support of politicians, the homeless, and abandoned children and deposited all in the Post Office round file. My body was responding to the nearly overhead sun and 85% relative humidity with my T-shirt stuck to my back and small rivers of sweat dripping into my eyes. But we had evaporative cooling as we pedaled down the street and casually made our way to Plantation Key and Luisa's house. With lots of useless advice from Luisa and myself, John quickly found the video.

"Luisa, that looks a lot like a sister ship for our Lady—isn't it the same model? Her finish needs some attention though. And they say she's pretty messed up below deck—maybe involved in some drug operation. Have we ever crossed paths with her? I'm sure you would have noticed."

Luisa replied, "Actually, there was a similar boat in the Key West marina. I thought of dropping by for a visit, but a thundershower and heavy rain postponed it. Then I got distracted somehow." There was smile and a significant glance at John.

I wondered, "If it really was a drug operation, I'm surprised they abandoned the boat. I guess kidnapping looked more profitable at the time, especially after they had torn things up below deck. Why are these motorsailers such an attractive target? It seems to me you've had more than your share of attention!"

Luisa interrupted, "True, but I haven't been smuggling drugs have you John? 'Course we were probably rubbing elbows with the usual suspects down in Key West!"

She continued, "And by the way. We need to get our Lady spiffed up a bit. I have customers—several businessmen have decided they need to have a quiet place for a conference. They will arrive a week from Thursday in the morning. They want a complete change of scenery and no interference from phone calls. They're calling it a retreat. We'll move out a ways on Indian Key Pass and anchor—serve up a good lunch from Krista's and have a good cold beer supply."

I discovered an invitation on Spam to join 350.org to protect the planet from global warming. It seemed urgent, but my knowledge of climate science was pretty limited. The Everglades City library is hardly the ultimate source for modern information but at least it is not cluttered with stacks of old books. Somehow they had been convinced to collect some of the works of the experts on climate. I found books by Hansen, Alley, Mann, McKibben, and Al Gore, of course. Hansen's "Storms of My Grandchildren" enlightened me about his experiences with the politics of climate change, details of the science history, as well as a few basic facts that had escaped me. This kept me occupied to well after lunchtime and I had to manage with leftovers—I wondered if Krista missed me. Then I wondered if I wasn't being just a bit conceited. Still, I thought I should check out the situation, so I arranged to get there at 5:30 for an early dinner.

Krista brought me up to date on the Glades Lady schedule. "Luisa was just in to order seafood supplies for the businessmen's retreat tomorrow. Her clients are staying at the Rod and Gun Club; the Lady is tied up there. I believe they may have been here on an earlier trip. They might even be the ones in the picture you had—you could meet them tomorrow before they move out."

Krista was delivering the seafood when I stopped by the next morning. The clients, dressed for a casual day on the water, had just returned from breakfast at the Oar House. The younger Latin types were definitely not the fishermen pictured with Orbatz. They were well-dressed successful businessmen. Even their shoes squeaked. Somehow their role seemed a bit awkward. As I gave attention to the senior blond fellow, he stepped past Krista, glanced briefly in her direction and with a smile, muttered something about catching grouper.

The comment didn't make much sense and I saw Krista give him a strange look. We hung about to cast off the lines. As they moved away she suddenly muttered, "That tall dude just winked at me!" She suddenly stared after the boat with mouth agape. "Just a darn minute! That guy was here during the raid that put my former spouse up North. He's a narc! They must be after the stuff that they couldn't find on that motorsailer over in the Gulf. And that's why Luisa's boat has been attracting unwanted visitors. Oh gosh, John and Luisa are in trouble!"

Krista ran to her truck for the phone. "Jake and Abner are halfway through the channel with load of grouper and trout. I'll get them to block the channel. Let's get back to the dock to my other boat. You can crew with Bart and me. And there's an old M-1 from the war stashed on board to discourage the sharks. Let's put a stop to this project before something bad happens."

We arrived at the blockade only few hundred yards out. Jake gave us a grin and a shout. "Sorry, but we're grounded. Have to wait for high tide. Got distracted in our navigation by a big cigarette boat out in the Gulf that kept harassing us. We thought they might be following us."

Luisa was startled by this organized blockade that required her to abort her outing. John gave us a puzzled look, but remained silent. The clients shared cautious glances; their blonde companion cautioned the Latinos to silence.

Krista explained, "The channel widens a short distance back. You can come about and we will follow you back to the Rod and Gun Club."

Luisa apologized to her guests. "This jam-up spoils the

schedule for today. Perhaps we can get a better start tomorrow, if you can stay. "

Back at the dock in front of the Rod and Gun Club, Luisa's customers reluctantly explained that their schedule did not allow them to stay for a rerun on the retreat. I suggested that we retire to the hotel bar so that Krista could enlighten Luisa about our reasons for forcibly aborting the outing. Krista explained over her glass of ginger ale, "I'm positive that at least one of those men was here in the drug operation a few years ago. I have to wonder if this wasn't a continuation of the attempts to check out your boat recently. And they might not have treated you very nicely. Suppose your boat has a load of cocaine?"

I suggested, "It seems to me that we ought to do a careful search of the Glades Lady. Who knows what she might be carrying. "

John protested, "We haven't found anything suspicious. Nothing extra in the sugar container and nothing stashed around the drive shaft either!"

Luisa added, "But why don't you drop by for eggs and toast at the house about 8 tomorrow morning. No need to attract a lot of attention from drug spies, so we'll take the Lady out a ways for a look-see."

The next morning, Manny dropped anchor for us at his usual anchorage out in deep water. John was in charge. "OK. Let's get at it. I can't imagine we've overlooked anything in the regular storage and it won't take long to make sure everything is clean. Then we'll examine hiding places like the anchor and the bilge."

Twenty minutes later, Luisa declared, "Nothing suspicious—it seems to be a false alarm!"

As we were sitting on the bunks, I suggested, "Time to

think structure. These panels are neat—but note that these screws under here have chipped varnish. Pass me the tools and flashlight please." Five minutes later I had news. "Ahha! Something not so standard here. I see three packages—here's one for examination."

Luisa remarked, "Doesn't look like the packages of white powder I've seen on TV. And this one is pretty solid. That fish knife there will work on this tape."

It was Krista who got the first glimpse, "My God! It's cash!" As she made her feverish examination, she concluded, "Looks like all 50s and 100s in used bills!"

Luisa stacked the package contents neatly. "Looks to be a few hundred thousand—at least. And there are three packages!"

John exclaimed, "So that's why we've been having visitors! I wonder how long we've had this stash!"

We sat staring at the bundles. I began to see the light. "I suspect the Glades Lady was mistaken for the Greenwich Lady in Key West. And the other boat came up empty and resulted in the kidnapping of the Connecticut couple."

"Possible. I suppose if it was a payment for smuggled drugs or some such", was John's comment. "You say that couple was from Connecticut?"

"I believe it was Whittaker, or Whitmore, or something like that."

"Right! Jay and Abbey Whitmore. I met them in Key West and they mentioned a sport fishing trip to Cozumel!" John paused to shake his head. "But I wouldn't have thought those folks would have been involved in drugs-—maybe diamonds or something. Guess you never know though!"

Luisa could only gasp, "Oooh."

After a few quiet minutes I muttered, "Well, whatever. What do we do now?" And I worried, "If we turn this over to the authorities there will be immediate suspicion that we've been involved in an illegal operation!"

Krista added, "And the cash will end up in some government account—I wonder if there's a finder reward. I'll bet not!"

John said, "I certainly don't need that kind of cash."

"You could buy another big cruiser, but that would certainly raise some questions."

"I wonder if we could divide it up among Everglades City folks. Looks like it would be a few thousand of handy cash for each of them."

Krista questioned, "How do we do that? We can't advertise." She added, "Ah, but maybe the Everglades City Council would need to post a notice: Be it known that Project Float is a confidential operation. Anyone discussing this with non-residents will be subject to house arrest and expected to host weekend parties for the rest of the summer!"

Luisa and John were bringing us back into Chokoloskee Bay in the Whaler. Krista had the packages of cash wrapped carefully in her rain jacket securely stashed between her feet. "What shall we do with our loot? Do you suppose these bills are all good—no counterfeit?"

I suggested, "We can take a few samples to the bank, but I suspect they're all good; the drug people wouldn't be taking bad cash for their stuff. "

"But we can't just deposit the whole thing; that would be pretty suspicious!"

John wondered, "Maybe you have a thought about where to give it a temporary home—some place where our customers with a bad history won't come to collect their property."

Krista suggested, "How about with our fish covered with ice? We have pretty good security, what with our boats and equipment."

Luisa replied, "That sounds good, I'll take us down there and we can move the Whaler around to the house later."

When we arrived at the Market, Krista volunteered, "Lunch is on the house; I'll join you in a few minutes after I wrap these bundles in plastic bags and bury them under the ice supplies."

We were well into removing the shells from the boiled shrimp when Krista joined us. Luisa wondered, "How do we get this cash into some worthwhile project?" Then glancing at the casually dressed group of seniors sitting at a table in the shade, she suggested, "I wonder if we rub elbows with your distinguished customers from Naples we might get some ideas."

One of the more vocal ladies visiting with that group asked, "Mr. Atwater, Sir, we haven't seen you over on the island much this season. Been busy counting all the cash at the bank, have you? That must be awfully tiring; I guess you must be coming back for the weekend to recover."

"Agatha, I'm not about to carry on a conversation with you unless you remember that I'm known here as Ben. And I'll have you know that a Vice President isn't allowed anywhere near the cash; I just write letters explaining why we don't just give money away."

ALEX COOK

I had been giving the C-note from the stash a hard look for signs of counterfeit origin even though I didn't have a clue about what to look for. With our banker in mind, I wondered aloud, "I wish I could tell if this bill I got from the bank is any good."

After the Chokoloskee folks had departed, Atwater casually approached and suggested, "Any bill from a bank ought to be good. In our profession, we do a pretty careful job in culling out the bad ones."

Then with a smile he continued, "I overheard your conversation, of course."

My sheepish grin was probably sufficient confirmation of my intent. He continued, "I got just a casual glance. It's probably good, but if it came from a questionable source, I need to see it in the right light if you're worried."

That possibility got me started on thoughts of a more complete banking procedure. Krista interrupted, "If you're on your way over to the island, you might want to take some seafood. Don't leave just yet. I'll give you a free sample of fresh grouper, so you remember where there's more."

John wondered, "Don't you have that little cabin and dock that takes up the northwest corner of the island?"

"Ah, yes. I have a bit more than my share of the island, I'm afraid. I've been there for more years than I care to count."

There were some careful glances among my companions. As I canvassed the eyes, I found a series of slight nods. "Ben, we have a slight problem."

"I know all the small businesses in this area are suffering from the sick economy. I can't solve such problems out of the office, but make an appointment with Audrey in Naples and I guarantee I will give it personal attention."

I waved a hand and shook my head. "No, we actually have an embarrassment of riches. We find ourselves with a large contribution of questionable cash that needs to be in use."

Ben hesitated only a few seconds and posed no questions about the origin of said cash. "It seems to me that you could arrange for any number of your citizens to contribute a few hundred bucks to a formal Float Account in our bank. We'll check the bills of course, but there will be no need for further undesirable attention." He stood with a smile, "Check with Audrey next week." I had to wonder if our expedition to the Glades Lady was as secret as we had thought.

With Ben's departure, we all gave studious attention to the spectacular dive of a brown pelican for a mullet in the bay. Krista finally announced, "Spread the word. Locals may collect a few hundred in cash from the iced storage for formal donation to the Float Account at the bank in Naples. The Float Account will be available for future Everglades City projects."

We began to relax. But Luisa was being rather exuberant between bites of shrimp. "I'm greatly relieved that we've removed the temptation for unwanted visitors to my Glades Lady. And it seems to me that our find is an excellent excuse for a celebration. A general celebration that is—I have in mind something for the whole town. How about a dinner party at the Naples Hotel? A fancy dinner with music and dancing. All supported by the green stuff under the ice."

Krista spoke up, "That should work! I predict a large turnout of townspeople for a freebee of that sort. Say Saturday night a week or so from now. Spread the word!"

Luisa continued, "Unless I hear a serious objection, I will

proceed with the reservations. But the hotel will want a reasonable estimate of attendance."

I wondered, "My Scottish nature has me concerned that we may have a series of celebrations at the expense of the Float Account. Don't get me wrong, though; please make that a positive RSVP." Then with a surreptitious private whisper to Krista, " May I be your escort to this event—and have the honor of the first dance?"

Krista gave me a long stare and a smile. "I will give it my most thoughtful consideration." Then after a brief look at the sky, "I am delighted to accept." With an amused glance and an intimate touch on my knee, she whispered, "I thought you would never ask."

About 50 couples of the younger generation were excited to join the party. I suspect the complementary invitation was a factor. We discovered that the older generation of folks was happy for us but were not inclined to party. They will be sorry!

The special nature of this occasion—my first formal date with Krista and the celebration of riches—suggested a splurge for formal attire with tux and the whole bit. But I worried that my neighbors would think that was an attempt to flaunt some sort of superiority. And I became concerned that Krista might not have a commensurate gown. But when I arrived in my conservative professorial garb driving my polished Prius, she stepped out in a gown that did full justice to a gorgeous woman. And with my bold welcoming kiss, I enjoyed an unusual fragrance of expensive perfume—with just the slightest hint of mothballs.

My dinner was the recommended steak and Florida lobster; Krista felt unable to desert her supporting industry and ordered the specialty of East Coast pompano. I found a wondrous enjoyment in the honor of the first dance, but then I lost my partner to a series of her fishing crewmembers and the fathers of Danny's school friends. Finally, with some slow music of yesteryear, Krista found a way to move with me as an extremely close and intimate partner. I nervously noted some of the members of our party beginning to drift away at about 10, citing concerns about babysitters and home activities. With some subtle encouragement from Krista's body, I bravely whispered in her ear, "The hotel desk person has agreed to reserve accommodations if we should feel the need to delay the trip home until tomorrow. I wonder if you might like to arrange with your babysitter to stay with Danny."

I was surprised at Krista's quivering response, degenerating into a giggle. "My babysitter does not expect me to return until midday tomorrow!"

I was pleasantly shocked and moved to stare into Krista's eyes. Then I found myself engaged in a long passionate kiss with this surprising woman. As we disengaged, we found that our friends had ceased to dance and were giving us lengthy applause!

We gave a brief look at our room's view of the Gulf beach. I was embarrassingly nervous about my long vacation from sexual activity. But not to worry! My partner was extremely helpful and promised a return engagement in the wee morning hours.

There was an interesting conversation going on in the DEA office in Washington. "Peter, it looks as if you screwed up on that boat search for drug cash. And the grapevine has it that the Everglades City folks have a new Float Account in the bank in Naples. What happened?"

"I suspect that one of the locals somehow got a clue that identified my undercover activity as one of bad guys from our square grouper operation a few years ago. But supposing we had found that stash: the cash wasn't going to add to our operating fund anyway. Those folks will find a good use for it."

Max stared at Peter with a suspicious look. "True, it won't be used to finance more drug activity. If your suspicion of exposure is correct, you may be in a dangerous position—and you're no longer of use to us." Max shuffled papers on the desk. "There is considerable need for guys with devious minds to ferret out the smart villains in the pipeline for government influence. How would you like a transfer to Sheila Michel's office? She monitors the lobbying activity relating to climate change. And she's a recent and very glamorous widow!"

Restoring the Everglades environment seems to be a hot topic these days. I seem to recall that the *River of Grass* lady couldn't make up her mind about it. But the internet seems to have found a new environmental worry: something called global warming. Of course that hadn't been invented in Marjory's day. And I can't find any Florida books that even mention greenhouse gases. News on the internet occasionally mentioned the pronouncements of James Hansen from NASA about the relationship between burning coal and sea level rise.

I wonder, does it make any sense to spend big bucks on restoring the Everglades if we eventually and inevitably flood the sawgrass with saltwater? I wonder what Krista thinks about it—she has lived here most of her life and seems pretty level-headed about finances. Big Sugar Agriculture and Palm Beach Mansions are a little out of her class, but is that what's really important in Florida life?

This wasn't what I had in mind for retirement. But it was a good excuse to visit with Krista at lunch. Since it was a slow season for customers, I was tempted to whisper,

"I would like your confidential advice about a very sensitive matter." Then a long pause, but I chickened out on anything personal. Instead I asked, "Are you familiar with CERP?"

"I know what the letters mean, but there seems to be a lot of politics involved in spending a lot of money to get it done. If you expect me to rack my brain to educate you, you really need to shell out for a pair of grouper dinners to stimulate conversation—but keep it clean!"

That struck me as a suggestion for dinner at the Rod and Gun Club some night soon, so I grudgingly agreed. Krista confessed, "You've been had, Prof. I'm confused as hell about that project—I just wondered if you would actually splurge on profit for the market and my personal attention." She added with a grin, "I was fairly confident about the latter, so you passed the test in good shape."

That stopped me dead in the water. I finally decided to match her attitude. "Aw, Shucks! Now I suppose we'll have to talk about my retirement income and travel plans for the future."

"Not just yet. But seriously, I have to wonder what life

holds for us here in Everglades City. Will the wildlife return? Will the fishing ever recover? Will sea level rise flood us out?"

"Things beyond our control, unless we can convince the powers that be to abandon politics for common sense." Then I bravely added, "But we're still in control of personal relationships."

This provoked a serious eye-to-eye stare and a long sigh and an instruction, "Down Boy!" Then she broke away to examine the growing cumulus across the river.

When the customers thinned a bit, she joined me with her bowl of conch chowder. "I overheard some telephone conversation that your landlord was due to arrive next month for an extended vacation. I wonder if you might be interested in some alternate accommodations if the rent isn't too steep." This remark was made in a most casual fashion, followed by a twitch of the eyebrows. "I seem to recall that you have recently enjoyed my efforts in the kitchen and certain after dinner activities, especially those in my spare bedroom after Danny has retired to his den." We engaged in a very pleasant mutual stare. She continued, "I wonder if you might like to formalize that situation for the entertainment of my neighbors. I have in mind a barter arrangement where you might continue to reside in my spare room with contributions as needed for groceries and the responsibility to transport Danny after school. No other commitment necessary, but you would be most welcome to continue to join Danny and me for dinners—and evenings together—if you are so inclined. Perhaps we could wash the dishes together." I'm sure my silly grin demonstrated my delight with this prospect of continuing intimate explorations with the woman I had overtly admired and coveted. I had imagined the possibility of the arrangement but was not brave enough to initiate such a proposal. And I really wasn't too distraught about the development towards a natural family relationship. Words weren't necessary to formalize the contract. We continued the intimate eye communication for several minutes with the additional promise of touching hands.

Krista apologized for a need to return to market duties. As she gathered the remnants of our lunch, she added, "You know, Luisa and John have given some serious study to the environmentalist-politician situation. We should start a casual conversation with them some time. And we could do some research on the internet. Sometimes you can separate the facts from all the nonsense. Like there was a good review of the situation the other day. It was a website signed by Orbatz—wasn't that the name of the professor you were searching for?"

"That's absolutely correct. A website you say? You remember that his daughter Amy was worried about his safety, but I recently had a message from her that he had just visited her in Colorado with a new companion. Perhaps this environment thing has brought him out in the open."

So we cleansed our palates with cups of Celestial Seasonings Green Tea, Krista's treat on the house. She promised to visit with Luisa about a late afternoon snack of shrimp and CERP discussion.

I'm finding it a bit difficult to adjust to the absence of seasonal changes in Everglades City. It's not all bad: the flowers bloom continually, there are no leaves to rake, and no snow to shovel. I got the full story in a late afternoon stop for gin on the rocks and a conversation with the bartender at the Rod and Gun Club.

"The locals even find that the occasional arrival of cool dry air in January is a welcome relief from the stifling humidity, and the mosquitoes disappear. It's tourist season: keep Florida green—bring money. But highway traffic is a mess. And if low clouds obscure the sun, the unhappiness of the tourists and locals alike is very pervasive. Finally about Easter there is an abrupt season change: the tourists depart. There is a gradual increase in humidity and, if we're lucky, an occasional after-noon shower to revive the grass and bring out the needles on the cypress. But one must expect a few lightning-caused fires in the Everglades muck and the condo owners on the beach complain to the chambers of commerce that the smoke is spoiling their investment. Then as the daily temperature hov-ers near 90°, there is a gradual shift from daily afternoon thun-derstorms to the near continuous rain and wind of August and September. It's hurricane season. Every storm alert inspires a rush for emergency supplies and all other constructive ac-tivity comes to a halt. The hurricane excitement dies away in November or so; folks breathe again and clean up the mess to welcome the next crop of tourists. One can even shut off the air conditioner for short periods of time."

So, in early July I was relaxing from the exposure to frantic tourist activity as I visited the fish market for a casual lunch of grouper and French fries. I was somewhat surprised to find the fishing fleet at anchor and the docks deserted. Krista lacked her usual expression of satisfaction with life: she seemed worried.

"What's with the gloom? Is everything shut down because the tourists have left?"

"National Hurricane Center says we have a tropical storm kicking up a fuss just south of here. Not a good time to be working out there, and we'll have to batten things down here if it approaches. The usual nuisance this time of year. It's almost hurricane season; it comes with the territory, don't you know. I suppose you are about to desert us for a quiet time in Colorado."

"But that's not supposed to happen until August or September. I must confess that I was thinking about enjoying Colorado aspens around that time."

"We can't control or even predict things that develop out in the Gulf. And the season appears to be starting earlier; might be climate change, I suppose. The National Hurricane Center predicts that it will brush past here and move up the west coast, then cross the state with some other weather from the west."

"If the forecasts are like those for Colorado, it might do that or just peter out. It doesn't sound very dangerous, though. But maybe I should buy some extra cans of soup and a candle or two in case we lose power, do you suppose? And some bottled water?"

"It wouldn't hurt. Then we will be ready for the next one. And that's a probable. You can record that as the word of Catastrophe Krista."

"Promises to be a not very boring summer!"

Sure enough, as the day progressed the clouds thickened, the south wind strengthened, and the sky fell in abrupt heavy showers. High tide in the Barron River lapped over onto the lawn, a good day to reread the philosophic wisdom of Travis McGee. But as the evening progressed, the rain came in heavier bursts and I woke in the morning high tide to find Krista's house an island with my Prius sitting in a foot of water and a muggy southwest wind buffeting the house. Cell phone contact with Krista at the Market was intermittent, but she comforted me with news that the storm was departing and the high water would drain with the low tide. So this was just an early example of weather in the subtropics. I began to wonder about future activity when the ocean really got warm.

Late in the day I discovered that my supply of Celestial Seasonings tea had been depleted as I sat listening to yesterday's rain. I crossed paths with Luisa at the market. "Good weather for boats and wading birds."

"Yes, I checked by cell with Uncle Manny on Indian Key Pass out to the Gulf. No problems, except that he's bored. We will go out and relieve him tomorrow. Actually I will be happy to have him come back here and hose the salt water out of our first floor. It's just a warning of the need to prepare for an August cat 5."

At lunch the next day, I loafed about with a beer while visiting Krista. "I see your fishing operation is active again."

"Yes, but probably not very productive. The Gulf is still choppy and stirred up. Not dangerous, just uncomfortable."

Colorado

I was impressed that Krista's fishing boats and Luisa's motor-sailer came through the storm with no problems of flooding or leaking roofs. "You know, if these high tides are a result of climate change, I'm wondering about life on a houseboat. I guess I would have to build my own. Think you and Danny might want to join me for a houseboat experience? Or maybe you'd rather just check out the aspens in Colorado for the rest of hurricane season." That provoked a bit of interest from Krista and an energetic discussion from Danny.

Krista expressed immediate support for Danny's travel hopes, but then realized he would miss school. "Danny, we have this problem: you are required to attend public school. And I'll get arrested if you don't!"

Danny insisted, "The internet has all that information and then some. Won't that work?"

Krista's reply, "We could do home-school I suppose. But you need to socialize with classmates. What would you do for soccer?"

I hadn't given thought to such details. But maybe—I believe the Golden West College of Education operates an Elementary School that is useful for practice teaching for their students. Best I call Susan Maxwell, Dean of Education, to arrange for a top-down enrollment of a sort of adopted son of Golden West's retired Professor of American History.

My conversation went about like this: "Susan, my

retirement in Everglades City has been successful in yielding a family-type relationship of the type that you advocated for me so unsuccessfully at the university. We plan a hurricane-avoidance visit to Colorado. It includes Krista's 12-year old son Danny, who needs to be enrolled in a public school 7th grade. I'm sure he would be an interesting addition to your Golden West School. Oh, and I must assume that soccer is an available recess and after-school activity."

The Dean's reply, somewhat abbreviated, went something like, "Congratulations, Prof!! Now you finally have a life! I must meet Krista and Danny—and I will personally introduce Danny to the 7th grade teacher and class."

And Frontier Airlines was happy to reserve a row of seats on a big jet with a photo of Charlie the mountain lion on the tail.

We arrived at DIA the last week of August and took the complementary shuttle to the Table Mountain Inn in Golden for a short stay. We had been fortunate to learn of a fellow faculty member with an academic year sabbatical who was delighted to rent his house for the duration of our few months stay. After a quick purchase of a 5 year old Jeep Grand Cherokee from the local dealer on West Colfax, we made a move into our temporary home on West 12th St. There were several welcoming parties by my former colleagues and we finally began our Colorado tours with a drive up Lookout Mountain. This was followed by my favorite day drive to Rocky Mountain National Park, over Trail Ridge Road, along the West Slope and over Berthoud Pass, to dinner at the Peck House in Empire.

I was lucky to be advised by an Iowa tourist that one of their early environmentalists had succeeded in establishing the

Cradle of the Wilderness at Trappers Lake in the Flattops in northwestern Colorado. This was a must-see for Danny, and the Jeep lived up to the nuisance commercials on television. Krista was a good sport about the cabins at two-mile elevation except to remind us of the balmy breezes along the Barron River.

But we were quickly exposed to one of the planet's extreme weather responses. An early spring continental polar outbreak was stalled over the mid-continent, giving the trapped energy released in the Hadley cell free reign to dump hot dry air over an expanded area. The summertime drought extended from the Mississippi to the Rocky Mountain Continental Divide. Danny was delighted to awaken every morning to the sunshine of a cloud-free blue sky, but Krista voiced disapproval of the heat and effects of low humidity. And I was hesitant to venture into the smoke-filled foothills.

My Florida companions found it hard to believe that Colorado's beautiful forests could be endangered by disregard of the danger of wildfires. I was forced to explain that the historical exploitation of the forest resources by individuals and industries was a situation severely aggravated by global warming. The management of the USFS continued to ignore the advice of long-established mountain residents. The high-bidder timber industry machines transformed the doghair lodgepole and undergrowth in areas of neglected forest into fragments of tree trunks and branches and mountains of slash to be burned. Deskbound civil servants in the flatlands promised that a diverse forest of replacement aspens and spruce would soon follow this destruction. However, this was soon nullified by the prompt eruption of more doghair lodgepoles, ripe for dry season lightning strikes and wildfire. The dry foothills were prone to ignition by nighttime lightning and careless campers. Fire season extended from April to October. My description of the air filled with smoke and the slow traffic caused by evacuation departures and neighborhood volunteer fire department response convinced Krista to agree to my suggestion of afternoon snacks of sourdough bread and goat cheese, marinated olives, and gin and tonic in the back yard flatland shade of Golden.

So we relaxed at Golden West; there were numerous dinner parties with colleagues from the university and a special Christmas Party. A winter storm warning with a high wind warning the first week in January was the signal to return to Everglades City. The Jeep was promised a comfortable parking spot with my friends in the search for Orbatz, and Albert delivered us to DIA for an early morning flight to Ft. Lauderdale.

PART II
ORBATZ AND CLIMATE CHANGE

Hurricane season seemed a good time to introduce Krista and Danny to the mountains of Colorado. When we returned to Florida in January, we were happy to find that John and Luisa had arranged for a new roof on Krista's house after a damaging wind in cat 2 Hurricane Madeline. There were a few roofs with blue tarp decorations, but otherwise the town appeared exactly as we had left it. Krista's fishing fleet was operating smoothly on a regular schedule. I splurged on stone crab claws for all our old friends at Krista's Island Seafood and settled in to cope with the Florida liquid sunshine.

I usually checked the internet every morning for the South Florida news of disasters in the world and stories of amusing recreational misbehavior of new arrivals in paradise. On Monday morning there was almost always an episode of shark bite or alligator attack. Occasionally there was an outrage blog from some tourist who has just discovered that the publicity about Florida sunshine, or beach bunnies, or flamingoes in the back yard, was a fraud. The one on Tuesday morning was a serious reminder that climate change was real and that we should do some careful planning about adaptation. This was a long-winded comment attached to one of the prominent climate websites. It appeared to be written by a wealthy incomer heavily invested in beach property:

J. Zorbat here. Bear with me folks. I've decided to get my 2-bits on the internet about Climate Change and Everglades Restoration.

When I moved to Lauderdale a few years ago, the weather in Philly was pretty awful. Snow problems in winter were off the wall and early spring rains flooded my neighborhood; even the Interstate was shut down. There were summer thunderstorms every afternoon, even an occasional tornado. Things were not that much better at the lower latitudes. I had seen Al Gore's red map of seawater in the Everglades, but figured that was a prediction for some time in the next century. Of course, I expected some remnants of an Alberta Clipper to make it all the way to the Keys sometime in December, but there was this 40 mph northeast wind following it. And my parking garage was full of sand and salt water! The Intracoastal was full and brackish water was backing up into the residential canals. It made me wonder if perhaps we should do some long range planning for disruptive climate change.

Now don't get me wrong. I don't understand enough science to blindly accept the idea that a few molecules from burning fossil fuels can change the climate, or the predictions from some backroom super computer that a few degrees temperature can raise the sea level by 20 feet. It can't even predict the weather for the next day. And the TV people keep reporting with equal weight statements of fraud by blowhard politicians to one-line summaries of some government-funded research published in some magazine that I never heard of. Those TV ads that I see every night about clean coal or the ads from the oil and gas companies are a lot more gorgeous than some college professor's explanation to a congressional committee on C-span about measurement uncertainties.

I didn't earn this 18th floor condo by scattering my pennies around willy-nilly. My Daddy left me a bit of a bundle to invest carefully and I was lucky that the general economy was growing at a good pace. So I'm wondering about the logic of reversing the course of water management here in Florida. The economy has grown at a very rapid rate for the past 50 years or so with the way our water supply has supported development. (This little downturn we've got now is just the result of some ill-advised excessive investments. Ponzi schemes have a long history in Florida!) Of course there are some aspects of the CERP program that I support. Water supply protection for the extensive developments of expensive homes for retirees between the coastal ridge and the freshwater perimeter levees is becoming critical with the threat of saltwater intrusion into the wells. If those properties go begging for buyers, my bank will be in a bad way with foreclosures. Of course this may just be temporary; this climate change may be part of a cycle. But I would be more comfortable with a little extra water; we can always drain the surplus into the ocean.

And I object to spending my state and federal tax money to tie up that sugar land in the glades just to grow sawgrass. This idea of restoring the shallow water flow to Everglades National Park is pretty naive. Sugar cane has used up the nice black muck and there is about 6 ft of subsidence in that whole area. Water on that land isn't going anywhere without a lot of help from some very expensive pumps. Big Sugar profits from that degraded soil are not so great anymore, so they will be happy to sell to developers for a huge new area of residence properties. What about this proposed Sugar Hill 18,000 homes development on 43,000 acres!!! (The sun still shines there and there's never any snow!) Just imagine a revitalized developer flying a third vice president for Peabody Coal down in a private jet to view a multi-million dollar residence in a sunny gated community. And only a short helicopter hop to the Lauderdale beach and dinner at the Diplomat. And of course, some hefty property tax payments to the State: got to pay those politicians!

There will be a few little old ladies in tennis shoes who will be a bit put out if those big white birds don't return to the Park to build nests because there isn't any fresh water to provide food for them and their young. But there are many more folks spending time in the shopping malls. And the water in the Park is already so polluted that food for the birds won't reappear for years. Cattails thrive on phosphorus pollution and look a lot like sawgrass. The tourists will never know what they missed.

That brings me back to climate change. Those environmentalist liberals who scream "carbon tax" just don't understand that abandoning cheap energy will bring the economy to its knees. Retirees will give up on sunny Florida if everything from soup to nuts is going to cost more. And any adaptation that we do to protect our investment here is going to be expensive, so we can't afford to stop burning coal.

So, wise up folks. Pay no attention to those crazy scientists. Better that we sit tight and wait for this spell of extra solar activity, or whatever they are blaming on spoiling our good life, to get back to normal.

J. Zorbat

Wow! My satisfaction with fresh mango on my bowl of Wheaties was gone with the wind. Some serious thought was required, along with a fresh cup of coffee. My first impression was one of suspicion that a rich incomer might be a bit prejudiced. That was tempered by the self-examination of my snowbird status, albeit not so rich. Then I began a more objective study of his various arguments. There must be a few of those new residents who had performed some lifelong honest labors to earn their place in the sun. They could rightfully be upset to see the saltwater lapping at their doorstep and being forced to shop for bottled water—or find salty ice cubes in their gin. Besides, the folks who mowed the lawns and cleaned the pools and delivered the mail and groceries would have the same problems. All those residents between the coastal ridge and the inland perimeter levee could be mighty upset if all their fresh water was diverted to Everglades National Park. True, that was the destination to entertain family snowbird visitors who invited themselves to occupy the spare bedroom right after the first cold snap up north, but Zorbat was right: they didn't know about the rosy spoonbills of the past, so why bother with replacing the cattails with sawgrass? And after Easter, the Park was only good for mosquitoes; real residents didn't give it another thought.

Maybe Zorbat was right: just concentrate on adapting to the present climate change. And it would be short-sighted to jeopardize our ability to get federal money for those inlet locks. There would be just about enough in the U.S. Treasury without disrupting the economy with a carbon tax. It must be a cycle; just hang in there until things go back to normal.

It was a natural progression to resume friendly conversations with John at the seafood market. It was easy to assume our early relationship. I began with my summary of past discussions, "Actually I've begun to wonder if the rest of the world is too busy chasing the almighty dollar to solve any of their problems. Even if the problems are identified, the response always seems to be limited to "Ain't it Awful!" In years past, one could hand out flyers about problems and get an audience, but now you would be treated as a nuisance and possibly arrested. So that method has been replaced by more efficient internet communication, but even that is ignored unless you can drum up a few thousand protesters in the street".

I continued to bend his ear with my words of wisdom that had been revitalized by my Colorado visit. "My published research never generated much response. Of course it never qualified as great American literature, but no one reads the printed word anymore anyway. For example, I'll bet the wolf-hating ranchers in Montana, Idaho, and Wyoming have never read Leopold's beautifully written *Thinking Like a Mountain*. I seriously doubt they would even sacrifice an hour of TV sitcoms to watch *Green Fire*, the documentary of Leopold's professional life. And the Midwest farmer has failed Leopold's land ethic in demonstrating the dominance of economics in land value. Every inch of land is planted and fertilized to maximize profit. Fence lines for pheasant nests are gone. Any other considerations for wildflowers or rabbits fall aside in the interest of market value. And I'm a good example of Leopold's complaint: I'm completely separated from the land—have never attempted to grow anything. Food comes from the supermarket—period!"

John thought to extend that analysis to Florida, "And economics has dominated land treatment in Florida from the word go. Drain the Everglades to make profits in agriculture. Build canals to get rid of the extra water and keep the tourists and wealthy residents happy. We followed the history of Leopold's learning process of mistakes and correction; we are just now beginning to appreciate an ethical attitude different from the almighty dollar. But the correction will be extremely difficult indeed."

I suspected that John was about to elaborate on Florida environmental work. "That reminds me—I wonder if you saw that comment about CERP on the internet, written by some condo owner on the east coast. Name of Zorbat—I don't suppose you've ever heard of him."

John just stared at me with a slightly amused expression. After something like a minute, I was beginning to wonder about the significance when he suggested, "Sounds like a character with more money than he knows what to do with! Did he make any sense to you?"

"Well, I didn't exactly agree with him, but it did get me to thinking. I thought that Everglades Restoration was an excellent idea, but now I see that it is pretty complicated. And I think he is about as ignorant about the global warming science as most everybody. But perhaps that website will stir up some people to pay more attention to the problem."

John just sat there looking at the water with a smile until a noisy airboat full of tourists broke the spell. "Oh I promise you there will be some disappointed soul out there who will try to set the record straight. But he will be in the minority; you can expect a flood of nonsense by outraged taxpayers." He continued, "You know, I can't think of any other situation where a degraded environment was actually restored. Usually it gets developed by someone who makes a pile of money."

"But the Everglades isn't good for anything but birds and alligators. The land is no longer good for agriculture."

"That's one way to look at it. But those property owners along the coast are getting concerned about the amount and quality of their fresh water. In the past they've had to compete with Big Sugar. Climate change is a much bigger problem. And they don't seem to realize that sea water is really their long term threat."

"But maybe that's just a cycle."

"Come on Prof! You must understand the science. We've already put so much CO_2 in the atmosphere that the climate won't turn around for another thousand years!"

"There must be some technological solution to correct it."

"Sure, just like the ozone problem. We corrected our mistake but Nature is taking her good old time to stop making ozone holes—they'll be there for another fifty years. Does your technology have a way of taking those chlorine and carbon molecules out of the air?"

"No mention of climate change on TV, or ozone holes for that matter. I thought global warming could be fixed just like the ozone problem. I guess I should catch up on my science."

"I've got to get these fish back on ice or Luisa will feed me chicken soup for dinner. Watch the internet for an Orbatz lecture about the Glades."

That triggered a brainstorm and a guilty twinge. Perhaps I should cover the possibility that Orbatz was floating around somewhere in the wireless domain. I had a little help from Danny about how to search. It was a shock: Orbatz has a web site!

Orbatz' Website

orbatzintheeverglades.com

Some of the comments on TV and the internet about global warming, climate change, and Everglades Restoration have inspired me to abandon my sabbatical/retirement to renew my professional activities on those subjects.

I. Everglades History

Zorbat's ramblings about South Florida's problems suggest a need for a careful look at the history. Florida's sunshine, beaches, spectacular bird life, fresh water, and black dirt had a nearly universal attraction for new residents, tourists, and developers to transform this environment into a civilized desert and immense agricultural enterprise. The secret was to manage the expanse of fresh water that accumulated due to 80 inches of annual rainfall. It meandered down the mostly flat peninsula, much of it in a shallow flood as far as the eye could see, or as a turbulent inland sea after an occasional hurricane. So, drain the Everglades for agriculture and flood control. Not easy, but with the philosophy of Manifest Destiny and the Army Corps of Engineers, the Everglades was successfully destroyed. The

meandering Kissimmee River became a drainage canal to permit cattle to graze on an exposed prairie.
Lake Okeechobee, the Big O, was imprisoned by the
Hoover Levee as a receptacle for the occasional hurricane deluge. Powerful pumps flushed excess water in canals through the coastal ridge to the ocean
for flood control, exposing the black Everglades
muck for intensive sugar and vegetable cultivation.
A slight overkill in the dry season exposed east
coast residential wells to salt water intrusion: this
was repaired with a perimeter levee forming extensive fresh water reservoirs. A minor consequence of
the project was a drastic interruption of the southwest seasonal flow of fresh water to what we now
call the Big Cypress Swamp, Everglades National
Park and Florida Bay. Particularly insidious threats
to these natural areas were the increasing concentrations of fertilizers and pesticides required
by agricultural interests, particularly Big Sugar,
to augment and compensate for the oxidized and
subsiding Everglades muck and the introduction of
pests that had no native predators. Loss of habitat
to residential and agricultural developments and
disruption of the pure water food supply has produced a 90% reduction in the magnificent wading
bird populations of South Florida. Florida Bay has
become a cesspool devoid of the spectacular fish
and sea creatures dependent on the nursery habitat of brackish water in the mangrove swamp. Some
would call these natural disasters collateral damage

for Capitalistic Progress with Economic Growth. Others have insisted that we have a moral obligation to care for our planet and our fellow creatures and now the pendulum has swung and the tide has turned. We now have the Comprehensive Everglades Restoration Project.

(Please forgive me for certain precautions in obscuring my present physical whereabouts. I will, however, renew attention to e-mail messages at my university and will forward appropriate comments in my future web discussions.)

Professor John Orbatz

I immediately sent a short message to Orbatz e-mail:

orbatz@yahoo.com
    To: Professor Orbatz
    From: Professor Russell Fairchild

    I am presently at Everglades City on retirement vacation from Golden West University in Colorado. I am glad you are continuing to be environmentally active, and appreciate your need to be discrete.

    Yours truly,
    Russell
    priusman@yahoo.com

I was in the habit of an early morning walk out to Chokoloskee, followed by a shower, and bacon and eggs for breakfast. It doesn't seem to have done much for weight reduction; perhaps skipping lunch and making out with an early fish dinner at Krista's Market would be effective. And the scenery is good! Ah, cell phone says call from Krista. How about that!

"You remember the other day we were beginning to think about the effects of climate change here in Everglades City and we wondered if John might be more knowledgeable about that? Luisa and John just came by on their bikes and I've treated them with shrimp baskets. If you'd like to drop by I'm sure they will be working on the shrimp for a while. We could start a conversation about the weather and climate."

"I'll be there in five!"

My cranking efforts down Riverside Road on the fat tire bike generated almost enough breeze to dry the sweat. But what's a little perspiration among friends? So we have another damn sunny day in Florida. Arriving at the Fish Market, I found the shellfish addicts at work in the shade with a view of the river activity. "I hope you don't mind that Krista has arranged for me to join you. And John, perhaps I could volunteer a consulting fee of a beer or two to correct some of my ignorance about climate change. I've been getting exposed to some pretty worrisome stuff on the internet. I suspect that an old Florida native like you has made plans for adaptation to sea level rise and more cat 5 hurricanes."

Krista interrupted, "But that's just for the next generation, right?"

John put an empty shrimp tail aside and wiped his hands before reaching for the next. "Well, we can probably manage to ignore most of the effects of global warming, but I doubt that Danny will be satisfied to cope with climate changes here for long—it will make the North Carolina mountains look a lot more attractive."

I gave up on the French fries in the basket. "That soon? I can see Bangladesh and the Pacific islands beginning to have problems, but no one seems to be worried here."

"Oh, it's business as usual here. The coal and oil lobbies in Washington tell the politicians that the economy must not be allowed to falter because of some hare-brained story of a warm blanket of a few extra molecules that you can't see."

Luisa interrupted, "John won't even watch the news on TV because of the clean coal and gas commercials. They rate just a little lower than the ones for Preparation H."

"But we've got today's problems to take care of first. The polluted water from the Glades is bad for the stone crabs and the fish in the Gulf," Krista complained. "Bad for my business. Maybe fixing climate change can wait a few years."

John cautioned, "But there's a problem with procrastination: adapting is getting more costly."

I added, "And this fellow Orbatz says on the internet that restoring the Everglades is hopeless because it will soon be inundated with saltwater. I think he means that we better save up for climate adaptation and begin action to stop global warming."

"I'm sure that you don't believe everything you see on the internet, but Orbatz probably just wants you to think about it." John was staring up at the clouds.

Luisa was giggling. Then she became serious. "My relatives in Cuba and Miami are very worried about the increase in Dengue fever. It's moving out of the tropics with global warming. I've been shopping for mosquito netting. We are going to need protection for sleeping arrangements, especially on the boat."

Krista was thoughtful. "I haven't seen much of the science but it's hard to believe that our country doesn't have leaders who are working hard on the problem. Or are we just going to have to concentrate on adapting?"

I wondered, "We've always emphasized economic growth and development. Maybe it's just too big a culture change."

John was slowly nodding. "I'm afraid that may be a fundamental difficulty. Professor Orbatz will have to give that some serious attention!"

I had only recently learned how to send e-mail, so it felt silly to check for messages. But there it was, a reply to my e-mail to Orbatz.

priusman@yahoo.com
 To: Fairchild
 From: Orbatz

Russ, I somehow feel we have met. I hope you won't be distressed if we continue our present relationship. And I have a feeling that it's not just my imagination that you are beginning to be concerned about climate change. I am forwarding a message from a former student. Check my web site: there is a lecture for both of you.

John O.
orbatz@yahoo.com

orbatz@yahoo.com
To: Professor Orbatz
From: Marybelle Murphy

Good to hear from you. I was in your Florida History class two years ago. I earned a C, but have learned to hit the books since then and I am now on the Dean's list. I'm confused about climate change though. Our politicians say it's a fraud but The National Academy of Sciences says that attention is urgent. Who to believe? Is a politician more intelligent than the scientists? Come on Prof—we need you!

Marybelle
mbelle@yahoo.com

orbatzintheeverglades.com

II. Greenhouse Effect

Unfortunately, there has been a tendency to ignore science in favor of misinformation and politics. The discussion that follows will be entirely based on observations and measurements; there are

uncertainties (not errors), but these are not large and will not invalidate the conclusions.

There is a fundamental fact about the physics of heat radiation that has been understood and accepted for the past hundred years. We use the concept of temperature to describe the energy of random motion of air molecules and we also find that the total amount and frequency distribution of heat radiation is dependent on this temperature alone. Our sun's energy and high surface temperature is produced by internal nuclear fusion confined by gravity. The Earth intercepts a small fraction of this energy carried by the solar high temperature heat radiation. The maximum intensity appears as visible light, but with contributions extending from the ultraviolet, beyond blue, to the infrared, beyond red. The Earth also emits heat radiation, but the amount and frequency distribution is characterized by the Earth's moderate temperature. The maximum intensity is shifted to the infrared; the amounts are small, but substantial.

The Earth's energy budget must balance. Of the solar radiation input measured by NASA satellites, about 30% is just reflected back out to space. The remaining 70% of the incoming energy must be balanced by the Earth's heat radiation output, which depends only on temperature. Using your laptop with the formula from any physics textbook, you will find that the Earth's radiation temperature is $-18°C$. But the Earth's average surface temperature is $15°C$. How do we rationalize this discrepancy of $33°C$?

We have, of course, ignored the physics of the atmosphere. So now we must consider the Greenhouse Effect. The snowbirds arriving in Florida have left behind structures with glass roofs that trap the heat to grow vegetables and flowers when it snows. (These greenhouses have glass roofs that transmit the visible light from the sun but absorb the infrared from the ground. Never mind the extra fans and windows—our Earth must do without.) Careful laboratory measurements have long ago shown that certain trace molecules in the air—water vapor, carbon dioxide, methane, and a few others—transmit visible light but strongly absorb infrared: they are like the glass in the greenhouse. Some of the heat radiation from the Earth absorbed by these greenhouse gases is shared in collisions with molecules in the lower atmosphere; most is reradiated in all directions. The downward part of the radiation warms the surface to a global average of 15°C: that's the pleasant 59°F average that we've enjoyed in the recent past.

There is absolutely no question about the validity of the greenhouse effect. That radiation balance calculation I just described demonstrates the necessity of atmospheric heat trapping; we have a ground truth measurement in our own back yard. An oversimplified view suggests that perhaps, with the exception of water vapor, the amounts of trace greenhouse gases like carbon dioxide, methane, nitrous oxide, and a few others are too small to matter. But the slight temperature increases caused by the energy trapped by

CO_2 in the atmosphere increase the evaporation from the oceans; the result is lots more water vapor and its very large greenhouse effect. And further warming decreases the sunlight reflection from the melting snow and ice and increases the energy absorbed by land and water which in turn cause changes in atmospheric or ocean circulations, not to mention the daily weather.

The upward radiation continues to be transferred by successive absorption and radiation. I hope you know that because the atmosphere is compressible, its weight makes the density and pressure greatest at the surface, and when the air is lifted to the lower pressure altitudes it loses energy in expansion and the temperature decreases about 6.5 °C/km (3.5°F for every thousand feet). So as the greenhouse gas radiation reaches the low-density altitudes it is no longer efficiently absorbed and much of it escapes to space. Happily, since the atmospheric temperature at that altitude is near −18°C, that makes that altitude the effective radiation surface that balances solar and Earth radiation. In the past, we've had just the right amount of CO_2 to fit with these atmospheric conditions to give us the stable climate that we've been enjoying.

The rather crude calculations made early in the last century suggested that an increase in the greenhouse gas CO_2 as a result of burning coal since the industrial revolution would warm the Earth a few degrees. But no one anticipated the effect of population increase on this process. This began to be apparent about 50 years ago, inspiring careful measurements of atmospheric and glacial trapped CO_2 along with global temperature measurements. We now know that concentrations of most of the trace greenhouse gases are increasing. And nature has tagged the carbon atoms in CO_2 so we know that the increase comes from burning fossil fuels for energy and transport.

Unfortunately, the increased concentrations of CO_2 and H_2O continue to absorb the Earth radiation until the absorption continues above that Earth radiation surface at −18°C. We have less heat energy escaping from that colder atmosphere and we no longer have radiation balance. We have less Earth-outward radiation than incoming from the sun.

So, is the Earth's temperature increasing? Global surface temperature measurements are messy. Various thermometers, observation times, and averaging methods produce noisy results; that is, there are observational uncertainties. But in recent years there has been a gradual increasing upward trend that is significant, about 0.8 °C (that's 1.44°F) since the industrial revolution.

And there are additional effects that demonstrate large energy increases on the Earth's surface. Glaciers are melting and Arctic sea ice is disappearing. Actually, ice melts without contributing to temperature change; the atmosphere warms more slowly because of the energy going into melting the ice. (The additional energy to melt ice at a constant temperature of 32°F is more than three fourths of the amount of energy required to warm water from freezing to boiling.) And sea levels are rising. The additional meltwater from the land added to the thermal expansion of the oceans accounts for the increase in sea level. These facts confirm the separate temperature measurements. And eventually, when there is less ice to melt, that trapped heat will be available to produce an enhanced global warming.

The Earth's response to global warming is complex. Clearly, when you increase the precipitation and the energy stored in the increased water vapor of the atmosphere, the weather will change. Hurricanes, tornados, droughts, floods, wildfires, and other extreme events will likely increase, but our laptops or the supercomputers give uncertain predictions as to when and where, just as they do for daily weather.

We have a lesson on a quite different matter from the past. We made a mistake in manufacturing some fancy chlorine compounds (CFCs) for use in air conditioning and spray cans. It turns out that the very reactive chlorine atoms and molecules destroy stratospheric ozone. As a result, we have the Antarctic ozone holes, and a few percent increase in global ultraviolet (and perhaps skin cancer) due to the decrease in global ozone. We fixed that mistake. We found substitutes for the CFCs. But Nature is taking her good old time about correction. Some of the chlorine is still in the atmosphere; the ozone will recover in 50 years or so.

The CO_2 story is worse: its lifetime in the atmosphere is even longer and the solutions are not so simple. Our planet's centuries-long carbon cycle involves the photosynthesis of plants, the reservoirs of vegetation buried in the soil, and molecules dissolved in the ocean and in sediments. The greenhouse effect of the CO_2 released from burning fossil fuels into the environment today will not disappear in our lifetime. The resultant climate changes will increase and the costs of adaptation will increase if we continue to rely on fossil fuels for energy and transport.

Professor Orbatz
orbatz@yahoo.com

I've had some comments to my website discussions. Here are a few:

Comments:
Albert, Tennessee Christian

I keep seeing the theory of a human-caused greenhouse effect causing global warming. Baloney! It's just things like the solar cycle or El Niño that are in control of the Almighty. And nothing you say will make me believe otherwise.

Beth, science student

I know you won't think I'm old enough to question what you hear in church. You can believe anything you wish but it won't

*change the facts. My parents shelled out dollars from their
retirement to send me to Gulf Coast Community College to
learn to think carefully about natural science and the human constructs of economics, government, and religion. I've
learned that the facts of science place certain limitations on
the way I must behave in paying off that debt. Consequently,
I have decided to join my generation in working to correct
the mistakes in energy production that those of you in the
unthinking older generation have decided to ignore.*

Delray Condo Owner

*Forget Climate Change—we've had storms with beach ero-
sion lots of times. And our Washington politicians have understood how important the beaches are to our economy and to
the retirees who bring money to our state. There's always more
Federal money to pump sand onto the beaches in front of our
condos!*

Hawaii Big Island Native—just passing through

*So you've got more than your share of climate contrarians!
You snowbirds from Jersey think politicians and Okies understand the work of God and really know how to benefit the
unwashed public. I believe history shows that we couldn't even
give that country to the Indians. And your TV people act like
the mention of global warming will lose them their jobs. Wake
up folks. You've ruined the Everglades and now your expensive
property won't be worth mule fritters when it's under salt
water.*

Ah Choo, your Yellow Peril

All you voters and those sitting on your hands, pay attention to some good advice. You've got big government looking over your shoulder at how you're shelling out for electric power from coal burning plants that put mercury, sulfur, and who knows what into the air. And they can't even keep up with the oil and natural gas companies that put oil and all kinds of other crud into your drinking water and the air that you breathe. Not to mention the Gulf of Mexico and the oceans. And then there's the minority that worry about the CO_2 that's about to make the planet uninhabitable. We have just the solution for all this. Buy solar panels from us. Your intelligent design god has given you more solar energy than you can ever use. And you don't have to dig or drill for it. Us clever Chinese have learned how to make these neat devices that absorb those solar photons and we've built nice tall towers that will collect the wind energy. We've done that while you've been spinning your wheels making speeches about who's to blame for the mess you're in. Send money, delivery is free. We'll credit towards those IOUs that are piling up.

On my first reading of the latest Orbatz message, I realized that my science education had been sorely neglected. But after a careful reread of the story filled with a bunch of new words, I began to appreciate the facts that had never appeared in the logic of the climate change deniers. A week later I was delighted to find another climate discussion on the Orbatz website:

orbatzintheeverglades.com

III. Global Warming

Society has made mistakes of various sorts in response to population growth and subsequent development. We have eventually corrected many of the environmental problems that have caused health concerns or even those that have resulted in an embarrassing deterioration of the natural environment. An important such project is the Everglades Restoration Project. The ill-advised pollution and disruption of the water flow has degraded the Everglades soil and the biology of Lake Okeechobee and Florida Bay, as well as the fresh water supply for citizens. In addition, the loss of habitat has resulted in the loss of 90% of the spectacular wading bird populations. It is generally agreed that investments should be made to correct the environmental management of this region. But not surprisingly, there will be economic difficulties for state and federal taxpayers in this undertaking.

There is a global mistake of far greater consequence in our exploitation of the planet's resources for food and cheap energy for increasing populations. We have initiated a long-term climate change by changing the radiation balance of the planet through the increases of trace atmospheric greenhouse gases such as carbon dioxide, methane, and nitrous oxide. The slight immediate increase in their greenhouse effect has triggered unfortunate amplification in the cycle of atmospheric water vapor, the major control of the planet's radiation balance. Other changes in water-ice reflectivity and in the carbon storage cycle of forests and oceans have increased the potential for major disruptions in the climate.

The corrections and adaptations to climate change are complex and costly. Nature's time scale for positive response to restoring the Earth's radiation balance is on the order of centuries, and our procrastination with corrections to business as usual is causing a rapid increase in the costs of adaptation. Climate Change and Everglades Restoration are not independent. The Everglades as well as the supply of fresh water in the Biscayne aquifer is particularly vulnerable to sea level rise. We cannot restore the Everglades without attention to climate change due to global warming.

I propose that our financial investment in Everglades Restoration be conditioned by our attention to control of greenhouse gas emissions. Costly steps to improve the water flow through the Everglades to Everglades National Park and Florida Bay and to guarantee fresh water to the coastal developments will be nullified in the near future by the accelerated salt-water inundation caused by sea level rise. Miami Beach is already spending $300 million for pumps to counter the high tide inundation of city streets through the storm sewers. Taxpayer funds for restoration of water flow across abandoned residential developments in southwest Florida and funds for acquisition of exhausted agricultural land in the Glades will be fruitless. And there will be demands on those funds for increased adaptation to sea level rise-generated problems such as the occasional tropical storm aggravations of beach erosion and the need for inlet locks on the Intracoastal Waterway. Long-range investment for subsidizing alternative energy sources such as solar and wind to replace the fossil fuel sources of CO_2 greenhouse gas should be given comparable priority.

Climate change is already underway and the business as usual procrastination and general population's ignorance of science will only delay our opportunity to slow Nature's sea level rise. Fortunately some local residents are beginning to recognize the climate change-initiated dangers of the rising seas. Some short-term mitigation has been planned, including estimates of cost and manner of funding. Fresh water wells from the Biscayne aquifer have suffered increased salt water intrusion with the Atlantic storms and the few mm/yr sea level rise. A partial solution might be increased storage of rainfall in a lower aquifer and improvement by additional desalinization. Some additional improvement can be obtained with storm surge control utilizing locks and pumps; this will also be an effective way to eliminate some of the canal flooding in residential areas. These improvements will delay the damaging effects of the sea level aspect of climate change, but will do nothing to slow the change or address its cause.

So let us not ignore the urgent need for control of greenhouse gas emissions. We should keep in mind that our procrastination leads to an increase in extreme weather events and disruption of habitat for ourselves and our support system of plants and animals. And there will be a dangerous sea level uncertainty due to the acceleration of Greenland and Antarctica glaciers by meltwater lubrication or a feedback melting process by the warming ocean water.

Funds for acquisition of Glades land should be conditioned by the need for these mitigations. The costly reward to Big Sugar for its depleted Everglades muck should be the risk problems of residential developers. And if we continue business as usual, there will soon be costly adaptations to climate change damages in the coastal residential developments.

The correction of water quality in Everglades National Park and Florida Bay is an extremely long-range undertaking to first dilute the pollution accrued from years of effluent from agricultural activity followed by a slow recovery of the destroyed sea life. This is in great jeopardy from sea level rise that will gradually replace the brackish water of historic sea life. Eventually, depending on our progress in control of greenhouse emissions, our fresh water reservoirs may be sufficient to embark on the long-range flow through the Tamiami Trail dike. The schedule for this activity is subject to a very pessimistic outlook due to society's reticence in facing the human caused problems of uncontrolled greenhouse gas emissions that lead to climate change.

Professor Orbatz
orbatz@yahoo.com

Comments:

J. Borzat, Taxpayer and Fisherman

What's with South Florida Water people these days? I'm not crazy about salt water coming out of my tap. And what have they done to the fish in Florida Bay—can't even catch skinny salt-water catfish any more!

Lifetime supporter, Friends of the Everglades

Who's in charge of those pumps in the Glades? Pumping more phosphorous and pesticide-laced water into the Park is pretty stupid. That's not my idea of restoration!!!

Loxahatchee Volunteer

There's lots of stuff growing in our wildlife refuge that's useless for the birds. What's with this project to clean up the Everglades water by growing cattails? No way are you going to break even if you don't control the use of phosphates being used for agriculture. And replacing the cane fields with the green lawns of housing developments won't improve that either. Come on! Let's have some strict rules on phosphate fertilizer from our environmental protection folks.

Latin American Visitor

I see the Chamber of Commerce folks from your Gold Coast are getting organized for adaptation to sea level rise. It's about time! We in the Southern Hemisphere have a much more life-threatening view of the meaning of Climate Change. Our food and water sources are currently being damaged; our very marginal standard of living suffers. We have been made aware by mountaineering scientists of the discovery of the warming contribution of black carbon production and are studying ways to control it.

A few days later I found another Orbatz e-mail:

priusman@yahoo.com
    To: Russ Fairchild
    From: Orbatz

Russ-I hope you have had some success in spreading my words of wisdom about our environment. And I'm working on climate solutions and adaptations for the next website post. Meanwhile, I'm forwarding the exchange of messages with Marybelle and Celeste, former students.

John
Orbatz@yahoo.com

orbatz@yahoo.com

To: Professor Orbatz

From: Celeste James

Thank you Professor Orbatz. Our Environmental Science Club thanks you for this Climate Change Brief and for all the other past service to the University. But, as you say, this country's citizenry has been slow to correct our mistakes in exploiting fossil fuels to get cheap energy for economic growth and a luxurious standard of living. The present student body here finds our outlook for the future very depressing. On the occasion of our wake for Jamie, our club invites the thinking members of our generation to join us avoiding the route taken by Jamie in coping with the future. We would like to take action for coping with adaptation to the disruptions of imminent climate change.

Celeste

cel@yahoo.com

orbatz@yahoo.com

To: Professor Orbatz:

From: Marybelle Murphy

Thanks Prof. But what should I do? I don't own stock in power companies and I have only one vote.

Marybelle

mbelle@yahoo.com

cel@yahoo.com, mbelle@yahoo.com
To: Marybelle Murphy and Celeste James
From: Professor Orbatz

Marybelle & Celeste—You've probably seen my last lecture—more info but no answers to your questions. You probably are a member of a campus environmental club. A suggestion for your members: How about a Climate Corps, organized on Facebook? You have perhaps read *Requiem for a Species*; the last chapter suggests some action for you, even a need for civil disobedience since our government leaders and corporate executives are stalling about carbon control. And the public is either ignorant or apathetic about the problem. I envision the Climate Corps as an independent movement by young people knowledgeable about global warming and climate change and concerned about their future. I believe you can quickly attract youthful members nationwide who have been frustrated by the attitudes of their elders. And there are some responsible citizens who will support you.

The Prof
orbatz@yahoo.com

As I reread the e-mails, I was struck by the contrast in the Professor's signoff to the students and the informal Russ-John for my messages. The e-mail suggesting that the John Orbatz of that communication was a longtime friend and that our relationship should continue might be an admission that my search for Amy's father had actually been successful. But there was also an implication that I should continue to be discrete. Best I continue this casual relationship with bewhiskered John.

In any case, Professor John Orbatz had moved out of his shell. And sure 'nuff, the next week the Orbatz website had another lecture:

orbatzintheeverglades.com

IV. Solutions

So, the scientists tell us that global warming is for real and is causing climate change. And you respond, "Nature has always given us changes in the weather and seasons. And like in the past, maybe we are in a cycle of increased solar activity with a little ice age to follow the decrease part of the cycle. We can adapt to these changes like always until things go back to normal."

Folks, you didn't pay attention to my last message. This climate change is of our own making: we are so many that not only are we part of Nature, we are the influencing force. And Nature's time scale will not permit us a return to normal, or our children, or our grandchildren. We were arrogant in thinking that we could exploit our planet's resources for energy and food without limit. And we ignored the warnings of those who explained that the slight increase in the heat trapping by very small concentrations of carbon dioxide, methane, or nitrous oxide might change the way water vapor controls our climate. Now we find

that there are natural laws of feedback processes where these human increases of trace greenhouse gases control the amount of water vapor in the atmosphere and change the radiation balance of the planet.

Let us consider an intelligent response to this situation. We can slow this process of disruptive climate change if we correct our mistake of increasing the greenhouse gas emissions into the atmosphere. We are aware that atmospheric water responds quickly, in about 10 days, to variations. And methane has a lifetime in the atmosphere that is controlled by chemistry and is relatively short. And we find that, molecule for molecule, methane and nitrous oxide are very strong absorbers in trapping the Earth's heat radiation. So we could make a relatively prompt reduction in the greenhouse effect by reducing these emissions. But reducing the use of nitrogenous fertilizers would sacrifice some important food production and the world already has a lot of hungry people.

So we must control the CO_2 emissions, and most of those emissions result from burning fossil fuels for energy and transport. We already have incoming solar energy that is arriving at a rate thousands of times greater than all the electric power generated on the planet. If we were to improve the technology of solar cells, thermal hot water, and wind turbines, our electricity problem would be solved. And there is still the future promise of nuclear fission or fusion for enormous energy production with no CO_2. Then we could drive our automobiles with electric or hydrogen power and use electric powered high-speed trains for public transport as a substitution for much of our air travel.

But now we find that technological advances in natural gas production are making that fossil fuel financially attractive to power companies. It is in fact also less polluting than coal, emitting only about half the CO_2 for the same amount of power. Those who understand the climate change problem think of natural gas as a bridge fuel in our transition to zero carbon sources. It may be considered quite appropriate for emergency backup to the intermittent sources of wind or solar, but it is not suitable as a long-term solution. Unfortunately it is presently cheaper than solar, wind, or nuclear, and this economic rule is causing delay in renewable developments.

Neutral carbon energy for surface or air transport has been introduced with biofuels, in which CO_2 is removed from the atmosphere by photosynthesis by plants or algae and the plant or algal material is processed to become fuel. Concern about dependence on foreign oil is the principal excuse for energy development of this source, even though in some areas it has disrupted food availability and cost. And now we need to replace the trees removed for agriculture and development. You see, the capture of CO_2 in photosynthesis by our forests has been an important control in the carbon cycle.

And finally, we need to conserve those large amounts of energy that we waste in everyday life.

The European Union and Japan moved aggressively to control greenhouse gases with solar and wind renewables, in part because they lack a domestic supply of fossil fuels. They adopted an arbitrary goal of 450 ppm of CO_2, thought to be technologically possible and predicted to force a global warming of 2°C. But with measurements of 400 ppm of CO_2, the rapid developments in climate change led to warnings by Hansen, McKibben, and others that a final goal of 350 ppm would be more appropriate. In this country, we find considerable reluctance to abandon the coal supply as our source of cheap energy. The fact that we have failed to pay for the climate damage with our electric bill has never been acknowledged. Politicians have been lobbied to argue that the economy would suffer if we regulate our carbon emissions with a tax or furnish government subsidies for clean energy. But the natural laws of our environment operate independently of these human constructs of economics or politics.

Professor Orbatz
orbatz@yahoo.com

Comments:

Sally, Canadian with frostbite

There's a rumor at the office these days that the economy is about to force the powers that be in our company to weed out the dead wood with early retirements. So I've been shopping. I visited South Florida many years ago and was impressed with the Everglades and its bird life and other creatures. Now I've been getting the Newsletter from Friends of the Everglades that suggests a changing story. Looks to me like they plan for a population limited to wealthy seniors who just want to put their feet up in their air conditioned houses and watch soap operas all day, then eat grilled steak by the pool in the evening. It looks to me like natural evolution is about to kick in. After a few years of sea level rise the salt water will flood the coastal developments as well as the Everglades. Then a series of cat 5 hurricanes will finish off the surviving millionaires. Filthy rich Florida seniors will be extinct. Only salt-water crocodiles will survive. I think I will retire to Costa Rica.

Bortaz

PESSIMISM WILL KILLYA!

And a LITTLE learning is a dangerous thing! Most of us have played with fire of one sort or another—and got burned. Those of us with smart genes don't do that any more. But there is a pessimistic saying that history tends to repeat itself. That's another way of saying that we didn't learn our lesson the first time—we are prone to keep making the same mistakes. And if it's a big enough mistake we won't have to worry about making it again.

There must be a better way. Ignoring climate change won't

solve it. So why do we seem to resist trying to understand it? Or if we're really stupid, we will let others tell us—Not a Problem, Be Happy. Or just say "Ain't it awful, it's hopeless".

Come on guys. So we got us a problem—let's fix it. Waiting for a miracle is not a good way to die. There must be a genius out there someplace with a solution. Find him and follow him!

A follow-up message from Orbatz:

orbatzintheeverglades.com

V. Climate Change

I'm aware that only a small fraction of our citizens who are able to read have stumbled onto my discussions of the greenhouse effect. And of this group, only another fraction has the science background necessary to follow my logic. And there is a large group of folks who have ignored the science of the greenhouse effect and look only to the weather out their window for evidence of climate change. They see an occasional heat wave or flood or tornado that qualifies as a weather extreme. The fossil fuel deniers insist that these are simply examples of historical events too numerous to list. Even the scientists cautiously admit that a hybrid hurricane like Sandy can not be cited as an example of climate change, although that was precisely the kind of weather that the IPCC predicted.

But those of our younger generation who have

been lucky enough to be exposed to good secondary school science realize that the laws of physics that govern atmospheric behavior are not susceptible to random or human influence. There is no telltale tag on a weather event that indicates a climate change of the laws of physics. Don't expect your TV weatherman to announce, "That's the science change in the climate that we've been watching for; now we can all agree that climate change is real."

And the science history has clearly shown the validity of the physics of the greenhouse effect for over a hundred years. This heat-trapping atmospheric mechanism is responsible for Earth's benign climate. That science will not change. But now we find that our numbers are sufficiently large that we have changed the greenhouse gas atmospheric constituents that the laws of physics feed upon. Now the increased heat trapping in the various geographic locations is apparent in our observed global warming. Melting of our glaciers and polar ice and the gradual sea level rise are overwhelming evidence of the measurements of temperature increase. This drives the precipitation and atmospheric-ocean circulation changes in the weather that in a matter of decades qualify as climate change. It is the validity of the continuous atmospheric greenhouse effect that we must acknowledge as the driver of climate change.

Professor Orbatz
orbatz@yahoo.com

Comments:

ADAPT OR DIE

Climate change is upon us. Never mind how it happened; that's water over the dam—or under the bridge or whatever. And the next generation will have plenty of time to analyze the mistakes their forebears made. Sure, technology could save humanity, but we were too slow. Now the problem is close to hopeless. The really depressing message is that humanity's gene pool is designed to compete for and exploit the Earth's resources for increases in material wealth. It's true that humans are more adaptable than other creatures and there are a few who have the brain capacity and imagination to respond constructively to bad situations. So do it!

Torbaz

These recent comments suggest that Orbatz lectures may be getting some constructive thoughts. And the subject seems to have inspired some local attention. Jessica Murphy is the oldest daughter of Patrick Murphy, the part owner of the Mary B, one of the fishing boats operating out of the Island Seafood Market. She is also a science teacher at Everglades Middle School. Danny says she has been getting some persistent questioning about the weather. Much of this activity was triggered by the back-to-back high water situations that flooded the soccer field. Brackish water in the green grass doesn't improve the game, so that kind of weather really gets a student's attention. I gather the discussion went something like the following:

Barney Kazynski began the irate complaints early on Monday as the water was finally leaving with the low tide, "Ms. Murphy, what's causing these floods? We had a soccer game scheduled for late today; now it's been canceled."

"I know, Barney. We just have to adapt to these weather situations. Temperatures have been just a bit warmer in recent years and the polar ice caps have been melting and making the sea level rise a few inches. Then if we have high tide during a tropical storm out in the Gulf like now, the Barron River across the street overflows. They call it climate change."

"But why is it getting warmer?"

"Well, the sun radiates heat to the Earth, of course. And the atmosphere makes the weather. The heat from the sun evaporates water from the ocean and then it rains someplace a week or so later. But while that water vapor is in the atmosphere it traps some of the sun's heat, sort of like a greenhouse. That keeps the Earth warm enough for the plants and animals, including us. And now there are so many of us humans that we are adding more heat trapping gases and that evaporates more water and traps a little more heat."

Ann Jeffries sounded upset. "But we don't need that extra heat. Aren't we making a big mistake? And why isn't all this information in our science book?"

Murphy was apologetic. "Yes, it's beginning to look like a serious mistake. But we've worked hard to make our lives better by burning fossil fuels to give us energy to make things. That's adding more and more carbon dioxide molecules to the air. They trap some of the Earth's heat radiation; they're called greenhouse gases. That's not in our science books yet, partly because many people didn't believe the science. And because the power companies don't want to change the way they produce electricity, there are still lots of people and politicians who just want to continue business as usual. It's an Inconvenient Truth, like the video that we watched that won the Nobel Peace Prize. So the mistake isn't getting attention."

"Hey, I don't like the idea of it getting warmer and warmer for the rest of my life!" This erupted from Tom Adamson as he stood with a worried look. "I didn't vote for those jerks in Congress who are supposed to be making rules to take care of us; I'm not old enough. What can I do to get things fixed?"

I gather that the discussion deteriorated in frustration. I have since wondered at the absence of criticism of Jessica Murphy's departure from the approved lesson plan. I rather expected outrage from some of the conservative establishment. Perhaps the shadow of Patrick Murphy's long tenure as a prominent citizen—and Jessica's father—was a factor.

PART III
CLIMATE CORPS

I had an inspiration to move things along on the problem of climate change. This e-mail message is the result:

priusman@yahoo.com
To: Marybelle Anderson
From: Priusman

Marybelle—I've been reading Orbatz' messages. I recognize that the organization and activities of your new generation to search for solutions to climate change would be a disruption of your education and professional career. But might your career plans be futile if we have disruptive climate change as forecast? And I'm aware that there are some young folks here in Everglades City who are quite upset with the failure of the voting public to move ahead on steps to curb global warming. Perhaps this would be a good loca tion for initiating Climate Corps activities as Professor Orbatz has suggested. Also, there are some local folks who wonder if we might invest in some solar or wind facilities to become independent of fossil fueled power, and make a start on slowing down the sea level rise that threatens to flood our town. (We have some considerable investment potential that floated in on the tide, so to speak.) We could use some engineering expertise from Nova students—expense paid volunteers—interested?

priusman@yahoo.com
> To: priusman@yahoo.com
> From: Marybelle Anderson

Classes are finished—time for some fresh air. So clue us in to the C.C. Janet and I have decided to get some kayaking time. We see that the Ivey House in E.C. has facilities and a room. We will be there this weekend. Look us up.

Marybelle
mbelle@yahoo.com

Oh My! What have I started? Not my idea of relaxing retirement. But could be interesting; I will look for them at Ivey House breakfast.

The Ivey House is relatively quiet in early summer. Mostly young folks were dressed for activity on the water. The pair of early twenties females sitting near the coffee maker gave me an expectant glance. I prepared my brew, then tilted my head and explored with "Marybelle?"

There was an abrupt nod and smile from the blue-eyed lass with the glossy black ponytail. Her companion gave the situation careful study; her analysis of my approach seemed a bit suspicious. Sunglasses perched on dark brown hair and functional attire with adequate sun protection suggested a mature no-nonsense attitude. "I'm Janet."

"Good to meet you ladies—I'm Russ, formerly Professor

of History, recently retired. I understand that you plan to do some kayaking—I believe there are some competent guides here. It's the beginning of mosquito season so they will probably show you around Chokoloskee Bay, maybe Turner River. My experience in a kayak was for a very cautious 100 yards—I'm not ready for an open water expedition." I received an understanding smile. "I believe we have communicated with some concern about the climate situation. I'm just learning about it, but I've observed that there are some other young people here who are becoming very anxious about their future. And their science teacher is rather knowledgeable and concerned about their frustrations. Perhaps you might like to visit with them and think about this idea of a Climate Corps."

Janet replied, "Yes, but I understand this global warming is a global problem—I don't see how we can be effective."

I nodded, "Yes, it is a problem for every civilization on the planet. And individually we feel helpless; we expect an entire nationwide government to move toward a solution. There would be immediate action if there were a threat of war or some pestilence, but climate change is creeping up on us slowly. Its damage will not be apparent until the effects are here to stay. So let us assume that we truly understand the problem and wish to act on a solution. What is the solution? Clearly we must replace fossil fuel energy production with an equally effective method that does not emit CO_2. Solar panels or wind turbines do exactly that and the energy supply is unlimited. We are loath to act individually because of the initial cost and the concern that the effect will be negligible unless everyone cooperates. (We find that argument used by nations as well as individuals.) But let us say that there is a cooperative movement by a substantial number of individuals who recognize the future long-term threat of fossil fuel energy production. I suggest that a Climate Corps of active members of our younger generation could do this. There is a substantial financial fund here in Everglades City available for purchase of the necessary hardware. There is an idea hatching to replace the existing commercial power for Everglades City and Chokoloskee with a wind turbine and solar panel facility in Chokoloskee Bay."

Marybelle was eager. "Really? Tell us more."

"Well, I'm just a bystander. Let me give Jessica Murphy a buzz. This is her idea."

Fortunately Jessica was up and about. I had a cup of coffee ready for her ten minutes later. "Hey, I'm just the local science teacher. Kids in my science class have been bugging me about climate change. I thought that some of the environmental organizations might welcome some contribution to their efforts to communicate the warning to their members that this was a serious problem. My comments to Audubon and others were welcomed but evidently consigned to a black hole: they disappeared. Their activities were their private domain; thanks for your poor effort to communicate, but no thanks. So I moved out on my own. I discovered on the internet that a 3.5 MW wind turbine can be had for something like $10K from every Everglades City residence and business—the precise contribution from each to be determined. Folks will understand that this becomes an increase in property values of course. There is a fairly reliable wind out there in the bay, and we could probably line the causeway with solar panels. We would need some volunteers to keep them clean but I can probably bribe my class to do that. We might even get panels on City Hall and the Bank building to demonstrate our dedication. Now if we could get Florida Electric to agree to hook our systems to the grid, we could have free daytime power, and grid backup at night when sun sets. Of course we could be more efficient at night if we got everyone switched over to fluorescents; we might have to furnish bulbs for them. But we need some experts to figure out how to do all this and some muscle to build it." Then glancing with a sly look at me, "And there's a rumor that some local cash is available. Of course Florida Electric will be upset that we are competing with them. They worry that we will be the beginning of a movement to decrease their bottom line profit. Convincing Florida Electric to cooperate might be a problem."

Janet was giving it some serious thought. "I know some young engineering professors who would be delighted to give some technical advice. And their classes would find this an exciting project. If some crates containing a wind turbine were delivered out there on the causeway, I'll bet we could have a crew from the university here at end of term—so long as you feed them and put a roof over their heads. But will Florida Electric cooperate?"

I suggested, "That will be a new situation for them in Florida. But I can't imagine they will turn down a new source of power—as long as they can somehow profit from it. I'll try and get some local advice about that." The Ivey House staff motioned for us to replenish our cups, then removed the coffee maker. That marked the end of discussion for today.

I arrived at Island Seafood just as John was paying for

Luisa's order of a two-day supply of grouper. Krista volunteered, "Say John, I think I'm about to help myself to a lunch of conch chowder. And Russ could treat you to a bowl if you will condescend to join us. Right, Russ?" and she gave me that gotcha look. I managed to change from a surprised glance to a welcoming smile for John. "Sure thing." Krista dished up the bowls and as I coughed up the necessary, she added, "Find a soft pine seat in the shade and I will join you shortly."

We gave full attention to the chowder for a busy ten minutes. John pushed his bowl aside and propped an elbow on the deck railing. "So Krista has me hog-tied for you: what kind of South Florida gossip do you want?"

"I guess it's pretty obvious that I've been bugging her for opinions that she thinks will be more useful coming from you, John. You see, I've been studying up on climate change with help from things I've read from Orbatz on the internet. It looks to me like we've got another environmental mistake to fix and correcting it is not happening very fast because folks think it will be terribly expensive—increasing electric rates, loss of jobs, that sort of thing. And this Everglades Restoration certainly needs to be done and it will certainly be expensive." At this point I mischievously decided to test John's reluctance to exhibit his professional background in such matters. "So how can we do all these things?"

There was a long sigh. Then with a resigned look in my general direction, he launched into a tirade about the emphasis in our society on economic greed that is disrupting our benign climate. The almighty dollar is especially paramount in South Florida to the detriment of the natural environment. "The early Florida settlers couldn't resist the financial exploitation of the Everglades muck and the water and sunlight required for vegetables, cattle, and finally sugar cane. At the same time, the wealthy visitors attracted by the winter sun were demanding control of the discomforts of insects, temperature, and water quality and quantity. And the natural sand erosion of the beaches sometimes led to disappointment for the weekend vacationer. So we asked the Feds to help by replenishing the beaches with offshore sand. And this is more frequent now with stronger storms and sea level rise. But the loggerhead turtles, sanderlings, and colorful fishies are not happy with the sand quality and distribution; they've moved away—or disappeared. And I must admit that I find the smoke of the occasional glades fires very annoying. But now the developers have convinced the Army Corp of Engineers to divert the unwanted water directly to the ocean causing the National Park to lose their fresh water life support. Big Sugar has used up the muck and is polluting the water with fertilizer and pesticides to the detriment of wildlife and even discouraging the tourists. And control of the Everglades fires is changing the sawgrass to brush. Of course we now have a healthy agriculture industry and elaborate residential subdivisions, but the natural attractions of birds and ocean life are almost nonexistent; even the sunlight is a problem with an out of balance Earth radiation." Then there was a guilty pause as he recognized my ploy to expose his Florida environmental background.

I wondered if John would confess to some definite feelings about the concept of a climate corps introduced in the Orbatz website. "But do you think that local activity will have any influence on such a big problem? Have you heard about our New Generation Climate Corps?"

John tilted his head to ask, "A Climate Corps?"

I replied, "Right! Jessica Murphy and some students from Nova University got this idea from the internet to get organized about response to climate change. Jessica researched a plan to move Everglades City to alternative energy with solar panels and a turbine or two out in Chokoloskee Bay. The engineering and business students from the University want to be involved. They hope it could be grid-tied to Florida Electric if they get the necessary cooperation. They already have a budget estimate and are about to start canvassing for donations."

John paused in his study of pelican flight and abrupt dive for an unwary mullet. "Ah, nice work. And the money is the hard part of course. But you know, there is a Float Account in the Naples Bank that is a natural for this. And there must be some well-heeled individuals in South Florida who could be persuaded to take an interest—you just have to know where to look. Maybe I can help."

Finally as John was about to leave, he made a casual remark to me. "I've been wondering if the water situation back in the Big Cypress has improved with these afternoon showers. Would you be interested in taking a short drive in your Prius to wander down that boardwalk a few miles west of here?" A slight pause and he added, "I'll furnish the bug repellent. Just let me ask Krista to hold my fish order on ice."

The Judge and the Senator

One of the Audubon volunteers at Corkscrew had suggested that I make a point of visiting the Big Cypress Boardwalk, but with my concerns about the missing Orbatz I had failed to make the trip in the mosquito-free winter. John's reminder of the problem was somewhat worrisome, but I couldn't politely refuse his offer. On Thursday afternoon we found the parking area off the Trail to be nearly deserted. Not a popular time or season for bird watchers. And the swamp was quiet—except for the persistent whine of hungry mosquitoes. Even John's identification of a bald eagle's nest was a disappointment—nobody home. But surprisingly, the viewing site at the pond at the end of the boardwalk was populated with a half dozen local Audubon folks who were monitoring the area for Burmese Python intruders. They had spotted a 10 ft specimen on the far side of the pond and were worriedly discussing some manner of dispatching the creature. They were happy to be joined by a scruffy unshaven character who volunteered to do the deed later when he could return with waders and a machete.

John was surprisingly sociable, with a smile and nod to the snake man and to another visitor who had a spotting scope trained on the one and only wood stork in the area. The stork man offered me eyeball contact with the bird and then continued his comments about the environmental history of the vicinity. "You know, it's hard to believe that in the 60's just 4 or 5 miles to the north and west of here, developers were selling gullible investors land by the gallon. The area had lots of inviting sun in winter but was a bit soggy in the rainy season. They had gobbled up the land after the bald cypress had been logged, and they laid out miles of subdivision roads and canals. It was a huge area and when the developers finally realized that there was no way for the utilities to provide electricity, sewage, and potable water, they just declared bankruptcy and moved out. Now the State has control, and with help from the Feds, is involved in a major engineering project to restore the natural Everglades water flow."

I interrupted, "That must be part of that CERP project."

He replied, "Right. And I have to wonder: if they close off all those canals from the big O to the ocean, there will be a lot of water for CERP to manage out here. Suppose the bald cypress will come back?"

John held up a hand for a pause. "You don't really think that Big Sugar and the east coast retirees are going to cough up the necessary tax money? And the Feds are even less likely. They are just beginning to adapt to costs of sea level rise along the coast. It's pretty much academic anyway. We're only 4 ft above sea level here and this CERP project is only a bit higher. With our business as usual climate change from burning fossil fuels, the Gulf storm surges and continuing sea level rise will dominate the fresh water flow. This whole area will slowly go to mangroves instead of cypress. Of course, the oil and gas companies plan to keep drilling back there even after it's under salt water."

The Audubon crew intent on exotics was ignoring this discussion and had begun to drift away. We were joined by the scruffy character who gave John an elbow and gruffly commented, "It's the almighty dollar in control again." And waving at the activity in the pond, "But these gators will always be here. That big fellow out there is trying to discourage that newcomer from moving in, and big mother has her territory staked out to protect her family."

John continued a friendly conversation with this pair as I moved over to the rail to photograph the dozen or so gator babies and watch the aggressive stalking of the 4-foot newcomer by the resident 12-foot monster. Later I noticed that the conversation had ended and John joined me. "Just touched bases with our famous Everglades caretakers. The scruffy gator expert is the disgruntled Florida Judge from years back and his buddy is a more recently forcibly retired Senator. Neither is very popular with the establishment."

I gave John a suspicious stare. "And they were the real reason that you wanted to be here, a friendly get together with your cronies." But then I wondered, "How did you happen to meet up with these characters?"

"A few years ago the Miami newspaper arranged for their investigative journalist to have a discrete meeting on Luisa's boat to interview an unhappy former Governor, along with the Judge and the Senator that you just met. Their unique political experiences suggested that they might have some special insight into much of the outrageous backroom politics and business activities in Florida—information that's the background for some of the recent unbelievable accounts of life in Florida that you occasionally find as fictional best sellers. You see, these fellows are generally believed to hang out in the Everglades and are definitely not accessible for interviews."

I began to realize that I had just been given an introduction to future activities with those gentlemen.

I was taking my usual constitutional on the fat tire bike Monday morning and found John and Luisa working at a leisurely game of tennis. They paused at the end of a game after Luisa won with a trick serve. John had apparently earned his only score of fifteen in a similar manner. As he approached me on the bench he explained, "She doesn't take kindly to losing, so I have to humor her a bit." Luisa just laughed.

John continued, "Any progress on that Climate Corps?"

"Well, the students that I visited with have taken up the challenge. They have a crew of about 20 undergrads and graduate students. They have an engineering prof and a business prof as official advisors and I will continue to work with them. They have elected our Jessica as President; the other officers are university students. They're about to start looking for financial support. Any ideas?"

"It seems to me that you have a good start with that stash from Luisa's boat. I understand that it's in an account called The Float, administered by President Jessica with advice of a retired professor from Golden West University. I know a significant part of it is earmarked for a wind turbine in Chokoloskee, but the balance might be a good example to attract some serious investments. I have some informal contact with a couple of the political types that you met recently and they still have some under the table influence with moneyed folks. Warn Jessica to be on the lookout for an e-mail about an exploratory conference on finances, say in a week or so."

Glades I Introduction

I passed the word on to Jessica, and then continued my pleasant habit of lunch with Krista at the fish market. I hoped to cross paths with John and Luisa there, but Krista explained that Luisa had confided that they were off for a relaxing drive someplace east of here on the weekend. I hadn't thought the Tamiami Trail would be relaxing, especially on a weekend.

But I had a surprise note from Jessica on Tuesday morning warning me of a tentative get together on Thursday, including John and Luisa, at a secret meeting concerning financial support, if her colleagues from the university could make it. I was invited to join. This was confirmed on Wednesday, and the Prius was drafted to transport us to meet the east coast folks at a remote bar near Forty Mile Bend. Jessica explained that an intermediary identified only as Jasper would contact us for further transport. As we sat at the bar with a token beer, we were approached by a scruffy local who said, "I'm Jasper; I understand you are the Climate Corps people who are to meet with the Judge and the Senator out in the Glades." I realized this was the backcountry character described to me earlier by the tourist photographer. He explained, "I've been contracted to take you'all to a very private meeting place out in the Glades. We'll take my airboat so's you'll have a place to sit with seatbelts. Finish your beer and we'll be off."

As we prepared to embark, I thought to contribute to the

transport costs and suggested, "I believe we should make a contribution for this service; do you have a standard fee?'

Jasper made an initial negative gesture and explained, "All part of your invitation from your friends in the sawgrass." But then with a glance back at the bar, "But to keep things confidential, maybe pass me a few small bills, just for looks."

The short trip was noisy and exciting and we arrived at the chickee just as described to me earlier. An unlikely pair met us at the entrance. The tall one with the ragged straw hat and week-old beard was wearing a torn workshirt draped over his cutoff Levi's ending a foot or so above his rubber boots. His well-dressed companion sported a bow tie with his tropical shirt tucked into his Bermuda shorts. But he also wore rubber boots. Our tall host introduced himself, "I'm known generally as the Judge—some ancient history involved. You can address my spiffy diminutive friend as the Senator. We will dispense with business cards."

The Senator was more vocal. "I'm Alexander Jameson, recently retired state of Florida Senator. I made the unforgivable mistake of accepting some substantial lobbying donations from developers and agricultural interests, then voting against their preposterous bills. Now I'm watching out for my health here in the northeast edge of the Big Cypress with the Judge, sometimes joined by our former state Governor. There is a nice deposit of cash in the Caymans waiting for me to decide how it should be used."

I added, "Yes, I believe we have met. My friend, John, from Everglades City, introduced us a while back." I noticed the Senator glanced briefly at the Judge with a slight smile. Then he turned to me and explained, "And of course, you may or may not be aware that it was John who arranged this meeting. He and Luisa visited here just a few days ago. We had a long talk about CERP, the Comprehensive Everglades Restoration Project, and the complications due to Climate Change. You must be familiar with the Orbatz discussions on the internet; it's all there." This followed by another mysterious glance at John and the Judge.

Jessica interrupted, "Yes, it was John who suggested we prepare for this trip." She continued with the explanation, "We are representatives of the Climate Corps, pretending to be well established business types, but we are really a rebel group of environmentalists. Professor Orbatz, formerly from our University, suggested that we formally organize to move ahead where our elders have failed to heed the warnings of disruptive climate change. Our companion, Professor Russell Fairchild from Golden West University, is presently retired in Everglades City. I've been elected as the President of Climate Corps. My friends from the University are Abner Johnson, the Treasurer, and Lois Stalker, our Secretary. Our members are mostly university students, but we hope to expand with members of the younger generation throughout the country."

Our hosts glanced briefly at each other with mysterious smiles. Then we were invited inside to a lavish table set with glasses of Florida Orange Juice, a token Appalachicola oyster on the halfshell—I understood that they were becoming rare— and Key West peel-them-yourself boiled-in beer shrimp. The Judge explained, "It is generally assumed that the Senator and I live out here—along with the former Governor. Actually we all inhabit one floor apiece in a condo over in Boca that we bought on a bargain after the parking garage was flooded with sea water several times. But we come out here occasionally to enjoy real Florida and maintain the myth that we're societal outcasts living like the historical Seminoles. We're powered by a small tank of propane that we bring with our supplies but we're planning to switch to solar sometime soon."

The Judge continued, "I'm getting familiar with those internet communications from Professor Orbatz. It was a wake-up call to me to learn that the global warming and climate change we are experiencing is generated by our increasing the atmospheric concentrations of infrared absorbing molecules that are trapping extra heat at the Earth's surface. Orbatz inspired me to study the work of the climate experts in their books and some of the scientific literature. And I've discovered that some of the science has been bootlegged into a few novels by some retired physics professor with the pen name of Alex Cook."

"I've always assumed that water vapor was controlling our climate, but I never realized that these other trace gases could be such an effective control knob on the heat trapping. And there's no question that the carbon dioxide greenhouse gas is being produced from burning fossil fuels to produce energy. There is a really nasty fact buried in the science that says that even if we stop this pollution, the global warming is here to stay because CO_2 has a very long lifetime in the atmosphere. But there are lots of climate change deniers out there who refuse to make a risk assessment; they don't realize that if it's really valid, the future could be really nasty. The author of the textbook *Global Warming* calls this the 'precautionary principle'. But I think the South Florida retirees think a more urgent precautionary principle is to spend Sundays in church and contribute to the collection plate with no attention to climate change. So it's high time that we had a Climate Corps, and your generation is learning the climate facts and has the energy to begin fixing our mistakes."

Senator Jameson added, "Yes, we have begun to understand the danger of this environmental problem and we're delighted that some of your generation is taking an active approach in solving it. You've no doubt observed that our human constructs of economy and government are at odds with the need to give attention to Nature's laws governing the climate. Our country's electorate may eventually experience enough examples of extreme weather to take care of a proper government, but it's going to be a bit late to preserve the benign climate that we've evolved with. And the economy has always shoved science to a distant second, except for profitable advances like semiconductors. But the greenhouse effect has finally reared its head above other considerations. The investment rules for supporting industries driven by energy from fossil fuels are no longer valid. The costs of adapting to this changing climate will soon diminish the ready funds for gambling in the stock market. And the rules for investing in safe situations with real estate collateral are being outdated. Intelligent investors are beginning to recognize that the savings from returns in free energy from wind and solar are a sure thing, and any encouragement to expand those renewable energy industries will move us into a new world that will escape the civilization degradation implicit in the climate change of continued global warming."

That discussion inspired a pause for some well-deserved thought. Then the Judge added, "I suspect that the Senator and

I might be able to give you some support. It may not be obvious but we have some influence, not generally advertised, on sources of finance that we think could be put to more productive use. I understand that you have some plans."

I explained that Jessica's Climate Corps had a project for Everglades City wind and solar power that was underway with some initial funds assembled by local citizens in a bank account in Naples. The Senator nodded to the Judge as if he had some special understanding of this undertaking.

The Judge smiled and added, "I believe I heard that a hoard of ill-gotten cash just floated in to that bank account. Good work!! That wind project of the Climate Corps is definitely a constructive use of it. And I have to wonder: was the Climate Corps responsible for that shipment of a few hundred small Chinese solar hot water systems that arrived out on the Miccosukee reservation? I know that Florida Electric paid the bill but they are investigating whether it was someone's computer hacking operation or if they have a mole in the finance department. But since the publicity was so good for them, they will probably try not to be embarrassed."

"Oh yes!" Abner interjected. "We definitely heard about that. In fact it inspired a happy celebration with some Miccosukee friends at Cap's Place over on the Intracoastal. Then we sent a careful note of thanks to Florida Electric."

The Judge continued, "I think it's obvious that human concerns about economic growth and corporate profit have dominated our political policies to the exclusion of Nature's laws of the environment, especially here in Florida. The greenhouse effect that is melting the Greenland ice and warming the ocean is becoming apparent in sea level rise to a few folks along the East coast. They are thinking about means of adaptation, but any mention of mitigation is forbidden: it threatens the policy of economic growth. And that controls the politics. So we have a very unhealthy partnership of politics and the local utility organization. There is essentially an electric power monopoly that discourages individuals from even thinking about alternative energy. And this has forced a small segment of environmentalists to identify our natural resources as a Nature's Trust that requires protective legal action. I just happen to be acquainted with a couple of old geezers on the utility's board who would be embarrassed to be accused of spoiling their profits in defense of Nature's Trust of our most important tourist attractions, the beaches and the Everglades. I suspect I can convince them that your Climate Corps activities in Everglades City will be a good thing in the long run."

Jessica smiled at the Judge's remarks, but appeared to ignore Abner's comment. Then she explained that with some internet advice from a Professor Orbatz, formerly known at Nova University, the New Generation Climate Corps planned to proceed independently of Federal or State support to introduce renewable energy to small local communities. "We hope to convince residents and small businesses to rely on grid-tied solar energy with hardware supplied by the Corps. Our Corps members will be trained in solar panel installation with final inspection provided by volunteer expert consultants. We expect the utilities will realize the need for the grid-tie to be there to furnish the backup power when needed. As the project expands, other communities will compensate for intermittent sunlight, feeding energy into the established grid. This procedure has the advantage over those huge installations in the desert southwest in that no additional transmission lines are required. We hope that we can expand the method to other Climate Corps groups to eventually complement those huge remote facilities."

As Jessica paused, I added, "That's the plan. However, we don't expect many of our Florida citizens will want to invest their spare cash. So our group needs to have an attractive lease arrangement available. We need to make our potential customers an offer they can't refuse. This means that we must be prepared to furnish the hardware and do the installations. These young folks have the inspiration and have the will but need financial support."

There was a quiet pause, so I continued, "And I believe that many of the residents of Key West have realized that the power beyond that furnished by Turkey Point Nuclear is coming from coal burning plants, and that is causing the rising seas that are flooding their streets and threatening their homes. Their business as usual with dependence on tourists is about to go down the tube with the high tides on the overseas highway. I suspect there may be some young Conchs who are about to revolt against the establishment. Your project won't immediately ease the threat of salt water, but they will understand and sympathize with the move to renewable energy. We just have to make them an offer they can't refuse."

But the Judge was concerned. "Our utilities believe they have been given the right to a monopoly on selling electricity and they may complain that you are a competition. But I don't see that there would be a problem of residents generating some of their own power—like you are doing in Everglades City. Perhaps you could just dispense with business arrangements—no lease. The Senator and I might be able to generate the necessary to keep the Climate Corps afloat."

The Senator observed, "Our power company realizes that they need to stay competitive with solar energy, and they are not ignorant about global warming. But they really need to take some responsibility for the climate change that is beginning to give us problems with sea level rise. They may be beginning to feel some guilt about their attitude of being happy that the government incentives for homeowner solar panels are disappearing and general denial about global warming. I think the Judge and I may be able to convince them to pay attention to the Nature's Trust. Besides, they should actually be happy that your Key West project will eliminate their need to invest in new generator facilities."

The Judge added, "Our mutual internet and University acquaintance Orbatz has recommended that we give this our attention. And there are sources of start-up finance out there if you know where to look. An example is a Canadian group called Corporate Knights who might be convinced that this is a good idea. I have a long history of slight influence with them. Orbatz has suggested that start-up funds would be appropriate. So, if you whisper sweet nothings in the Senator's ear, I believe we may get the show on the road."

The Senator added, "Yes, I believe I can lay my hands on some cash in a matter of hours. So I'll be prepared to spring for a free initial shipment of solar panels that the Chinese have subsidized. This will actually serve to compensate the Key West folks for their increasing costs of adaptation. Their desalinated water from the mainland is costing more and they have begun construction of rainwater cisterns, and flooding at high tide is forcing them to build sandbag levees or move houses up on stilts."

Jessica added, "I've actually had some correspondence with members of that new generation in Key West with references to Orbatz' website and information about our plans in Everglades City. They've been having problems educating their elders and getting the attention of the utilities. I think they are about to move independently."

I became aware that I was sitting with mouth agape, and promptly expressed my approval of the Senator's overture to the Climate Corps with a huge smile. Jessica gushed a formal thank you and promised that the Corps would make prompt preparations to move ahead in the Conch Republic.

Jessica raised a hand to say, "One more thing. If we can demonstrate success in this start-up, we will work to expand our Climate Corps anyplace we can generate interest. I've been collecting some Friends on Facebook and getting some response from around the state. This has the potential to start activities all over the country—and maybe the world!"

Abner added, "I've already managed a slight expansion. During Spring Break, I initiated a little project with my grandparents in Chicago. I visited them at their retirement home in the Phoenix suburbs and convinced them to reduce their emissions of CO_2. I demonstrated that their emissions at 10 lb CO_2 per dollar of energy use were putting about 5 tons of CO_2 in the air every year. It convinced them that they didn't want to know how many little IR absorbers were working up there, trapping extra heat for the next few centuries. They have now invested $10,000 in a solar garden for partial credit on their power bill. This was a divestment from Exxon at 8-10% to a new solar 4% return. They will lose the use of their principle for a few years, but for them it's not a problem. And it's safe: solar is a sure thing and fossil is getting risky. Then I painted their roof white, changed all the lights to LEDs, and put all their electronics on standby timers for another few hundred bucks savings a year and more CO_2 reduction. Now they're thinking about installing solar hot water to pay for using their new electric car. They should be getting close to zero greenhouse emissions. Their withdrawal from bank savings and other investments may be recoverable in a property sales settlement, or at worst a reduction in my inheritance. I had a 3-week vacation in the sun with an outlay of only about $100 beyond airfare. I hope now to convince other Corps members to do similar projects with their parents and grandparents."

The Senator responded with applause and, "Good work!" Then a pause. "Just one more thing though. You may not realize how awkward it might be to have Everglades City swarming with students from Orbatz' university. I have reason to believe that it would be a healthier situation for the central office for the New Generation Climate Corp to be elsewhere. I hereby offer the west half of my condo for office space. You will forgive me if I continue to enjoy the ocean view to the east."

I found this to be slightly puzzling. But I slowly realized that the Senator's smile in my direction might suggest support of any need to be suspicious of John's true identity.

My extended lunch on Saturday found a special treat to go with my Coors Light. Big mother manatee and her small child were basking a few yards from the dock in the quiet time between tourist airboat excursions. The youngster was begging for attention from his sluggish mother. My camera was stored in the Prius and was therefore useless; this image had to be stored in my mind's eye.

I was briefly distracted from the manatee display by the sound of a heavy engine that proved to be a tour bus from a cruise liner in Tampa. My glance back at the tidal river caught the slow submerging of the manatee family. I decided this disturbance of the peace demanded my attention and I took the last swallow of beer and mounted my bike to follow the diesel fumes through town to the entrance to Everglades National Park. I found the small crowd clustered around their guide at the park ranger station. He had finished the instructions for the boat trip into the bay and was beginning to introduce an extravagantly dressed individual who had just disembarked from a limousine.

"And we have the pleasure today of meeting with an emissary from the Gulf Coast Chamber of Commerce. He will deliver a message pertaining to our future environmental attractions."

I missed the mumbled introduction but heard the following tirade. "Today you will find the undisturbed attractions of South Florida. And you will find a citizenry content with this quaint little city. But I am here today to warn you of the undesirable changes in store for its future. Some of the disruptive elements of the younger generation have made plans to build an unsightly wind turbine in our beautiful Chokoloskee Bay. This was instigated by that rabblerousing Professor Orbatz who lives out in the Everglades. I think it's high time we get back to our old west custom of a wanted dead or alive poster for this outlaw. His seditious activities are an extreme threat to South Florida's economy and luxurious way of life."

Krista had warned me that there were such characters lurking in the gated golf course developments, but this was a shock. However, we were not to enjoy further explanations of our misbehaviors. One of our old-timer fishermen elbowed his way through the tourists to interrupt. "Shut off that garbage! You've destroyed the Everglades wildlife with your water management so you could plant huge mansions in the sun. And you plan to be the very last person to see the rising seas inundate the area. The rest of us and these ignorant visitors can just float away. Maybe we'll just have to convince the Seminoles that it's time to reclaim their land for the birds and alligators. Now Git!"

Our local spokesman was joined by a small contingent of scruffy fishermen and handymen carrying an assortment of fish heads and overripe vegetables. The audience was hustled aboard the tour boat and the limousine was made available to shelter the obnoxious speaker from the rain of juicy projectiles.

While laying in a new supply of pole beans at the market, I overheard a pair of locals comparing experiences on the internet. Facebook was mentioned numerous times; sounded like that was their sole activity at the computer. But it wasn't trivial stuff. Much of the dialogue had to do with the political situation in Syria, but they also commented on recent sightings at Audubon Corkscrew Sanctuary. I got the feeling that life is passing me by. I suspect that my Dell would clue me in about how get involved, and if I needed advice, perhaps Krista—ah, but I'm sure Danny is the expert. I needed to talk to Jessica about her experiences with her Facebook friends. So I was waiting with an order of stone crab claws to share when she dropped by for a snack after school. "So Jessica, tell me about the Climate Corps on Facebook. How does it work?"

"Okay. But I need to finish this claw with the mustard sauce—can't imagine how you knew this would help me to visit about Facebook." She wiped fingers on a paper towel and opened her laptop. "Here are a few of the postings:"

Miriam, Sun-Sentinel reporter

We haven't heard from Orbatz for some time, so my editor has given me an assignment to get a personal interview and pictures of the professor. His university informed me that he hasn't returned from his sabbatical and that his favorite habitat is the Everglades. Help!

Billy, helpful Miccosukee

I suggest that you visit GPS coordinates 25° 55' 47.25"N/81°14'18.05"W for Orbatz' sabbatical research.

Zachary, meteorology student

I'm a student at University of West Florida in Pensacola. We had a visitor from another near-by university in our meteorology class to explain atmospheric heat trapping. He said that the green-house gas molecules absorb certain infrared wave-lengths of heat energy from the Earth, and this energy is reradiated in all directions with the part going downward supplying the energy back to the ground. This Earth's warm radiation blanket gives us the climate that we've all evolved with.

Sarah, Key West student

In our physics class here at Key West Community College, we have concentrated on understanding the science of global warming and climate change. We have demonstrated that our greenhouse effect is unique in our solar system. We made the calculation suggested by Orbatz and found the Earth's radiation temperature to be 33°C less than the measured sur-face temperature, so we must have an atmospheric greenhouse effect for explanation. We did a similar calculation for Mars and Venus by adjusting the solar intensity for the radius of their orbits. We found that the radiation temperature on Mars is exactly equal to the measured surface temperature, indicating there is no greenhouse effect because there is very little atmosphere. For Venus we found the surface temper-ature is about 500°C greater than the radiation tem-perature: there is a huge greenhouse effect due to a thick atmosphere of CO_2!

Basil, geology student

Have your professors explained to you why they ignored the heat absorption of the natural water vapor—and what about all that nitrogen and oxygen?

Chris Baldwin, Environmental Research Fellow

I hope that you will permit some input from Colorado's Golden West University on this subject. Our occasional extreme weather manifested by canyon floods and forest wildfires has given us pause to reexamine our bad habits of energy production. Professor Mandryka has explained to us that the rotation and vibration energy structure of the greenhouse gas molecules fits nicely with the infrared photon's energy, and these molecules have an electric dipole that efficiently absorbs the radiation. That doesn't work for nitrogen and oxygen. I must agree with Basil that water vapor is indeed the major atmospheric trap of heat radiation from the Earth, but the increasing absorption by carbon dioxide has been called the control knob on the thermostat that determines the slight additional warming of the ocean by the CO_2 and the resultant increase in a lot of evaporated water vapor greenhouse gas.

Ann, Columbia graduate student

I am a member of Hansen's original A-team here at Columbia. You need to give more attention to the future climate, like Professor Jim wrote about in *Storms of my Grandchildren*. I'm sure you are aware that the water evaporation and precipitation cycle makes the atmospheric water vapor lifetime about 10 days. But CO_2 has an atmospheric cycle of forest photosynthesis and decay with lifetime of about a century or so. And the trapping and emission cycles of the oceans and soil are much longer. The CO_2 that we dump into the atmosphere today will continue to heat the Earth for centuries. And Susan Solomon says it won't let the warmer oceans cool for maybe a thousand years. We can't go back to yesterday's pleasant climate.

Corey at Florida Southern

We hope that religious institutions will take a positive view on Climate mitigation. There are no mentions of the greenhouse effect or climate change in the Bible, but the Christian rule to love our neighbor means that we must care for the global climate. In any case, the logical personal outlook is to care for our home. Professor Houghton has elaborated on a risk assessment in his textbook *Global Warming*. The Pope has made our duty clear. And Professor Hayhoe, with her evangelical Christian viewpoint, has elaborated on the science. Our physics prof says that Atomic Scientists have recently added climate change to their concern about Doomsday. It won't happen in a matter of hours or days, but it will be irreversible. "Natural Laws are non-negotiable."

Chokoloskee Turbine

The walls near the entrance to the Island Seafood Market were always adorned with notices of the current seafood availability, like Catch of the Day, the usual Conch Chowder, and the intermittent Stone Crab Claws. A new bulletin suggested that check donations to the Climate Corps wind turbine project could be addressed to Jessica Murphy, President, Climate Corps. And the steady stream of traffic in the direction of the stash of cash under the ice in the warehouse produced the side benefit of customers keeping Krista busy. The conversations around the picnic tables were largely speculation on the transport and construction techniques of said turbines. The fishermen crews were generally authoritative about the possible arrival of barges loaded with turbine blades and towers. The pessimistic comments by townspeople were carefully considered; perhaps some additional dredging would be necessary.

In a few weeks there was an influx of husky university students ready to follow the drawings by experts in the turbine industry for construction of the concrete turbine platform. Shortly thereafter the first in a series of flatbed trucks arrived with turbine tower sections. A crane specialist from Miami arrived to offer advice and assistance, but the landing of a large helicopter at the airstrip on the Chokoloskee road sent him grumbling back to the city. In the following days there was little business activity in town; most folks were parked along the causeway to watch the tower assembly. And the school and every shop were closed when the generators and turbine blades were hoisted from the flatbeds to the towers. The promises of turbine workers of early juice from the wind were applauded, but the continued electrical work was viewed with impatience.

I made an attempt to be casual about the whole operation, with my standard order of conch chowder and beer; Krista was amused. Then one day she appeared in the kitchen with a T-shirt closely adhering to her womanhood; it proclaimed her as Island Woman. She introduced me to a bearded fellow in calico shirt, tattered overalls, and dilapidated straw hat. "I want you to meet a fellow fisherman from Goodland. He just dropped by to make me a gift of this sexy shirt and to see how our turbine project is coming along."

"My name's Orville. I have apologized to Krista for not bringing some of WOMAN'S expensive jewelry. Some of the young folks over my way said I should be paying attention to sea level rise and climate change and should get educated about what your Climate Corps was doing about it. I think maybe we have some Climate Corp members who are going to insist that Goodland follow your Everglades City example."

The school day was about to end, so I offered to pick up Jessica and give Orville an on-site explanation of the work. Orville countered with, "The turbine looks good and I understand some solar panels are on the way. Our discussions with Florida Electric are making us lean toward a combination of solar and wind so we would have a more steady input to our power and less variation in demand from the grid. We're making plans, but we have to hope the Climate Corps will find the necessary bucks for us to get started."

Orville suggested that Krista and I sample a dinner at the Old Marco Inn. On that occasion we learned that the building had arrived in sections down the back road from Marco. It seems that its structure didn't mesh with the developer's concept of a modern residential subdivision. The food was passable although the view of the bay didn't compare to the Barron River. Our voluble waiter confided that the roof was due for solar panels, and a modest wind turbine suitable to Audubon was about to appear in the bay. Evidently the Climate Corps had been able to expand its work to our neighboring community.

As we sampled Old Marco's peculiar idea of key lime pie, we observed the arrival of a pair of casually dressed businessmen, escorted by a carefully attired young man wearing a jacket sporting a Nova University logo. As Krista and I moved to the bar for an after dinner liqueur we overheard mention of a Climate Corps energy project. With appropriate loitering in the bar, we were able to intercept the jacket person to discover the Climate Corps plans for Marco Island. "Those folks on Marco have been slightly embarrassed to discover their poor cousins here in Goodland are moving ahead on an energy project that looks interesting. They don't like to be left out of an attractive business project that would earn them more savings from free energy than from savings accounts. They have moved ahead of Goodland in that they have solar gardens as roofs on every parking lot at their shopping malls and apartment complexes. This was accomplished initially by the rental apartment and condo facilities that made solar energy an attractive part of the housing arrangements. The shopping malls made the offer of free solar energy for their tenants. And I've promised to give their Chamber of Commerce folks a good feeling by educating the retired folks about climate change in a series of town hall meetings."

As I was pedaling my fat tire bike along the causeway for morning exercise last Monday, I noted a couple of fellows having a bit of trouble with the brakes on their vehicle as they were about to launch their small outboard. They exhibited a somewhat extreme tan for local folks; maybe fishermen from back in the Glades. I thought to help in some way.

"Yes, if you could help block the car wheels as we get the boat off the trailer, it would help a lot. Back home our island is only a few inches above the ocean—not such a problem."

I wondered, as they spoke excellent English. "Oh, where is that?"

"We've just arrived from the Marshall Islands in the Pacific. Your government has helped us move here to escape the sea level rise that is demolishing our houses. The emission of CO_2 greenhouse gas from energy production in the industrial countries is destroying our homeland. Our Compact of Free Association with the U.S. after the Second World War gave us permission to come live in Everglades City. We're living in those small places just down the road. Now we're out to catch a few fish for dinner for our families."

I had, in fact, heard of the sea level problems for Pacific islanders. Their problems were about the same as our folks in the Keys. Houses were being elevated on stilts, but eventually would have to be abandoned. With this future in mind, I commented, "But you must know that Everglades City will also be inundated."

"Yes. That is why we will start on a boat city in Chokoloskee Bay. We have many families ready to move here as it grows. It is to be called the New Marshall Republic of the U.S."

I had seen warnings that there would be immigration problems cause by sea level rise but I was so astonished at this development that I departed without further comment.

Congressman Beasley

The new batch of medium stone crab claws was depleting the contents of my billfold at lunchtime on Tuesday when I heard a rather formal introduction. "A very good Florida day to you, Madam. I'm about to make a special order of your gorgeous stone crab claws for my special guest. May I introduce Congressman Beasley, who is your Representative in Washington? We have taken advantage of this Fall Recess to visit with our constituents in this unique spot of Paradise. And I have an informative poster for convenient display in the hall way outside to enable the citizens of your community to learn of Congressman Beasley's activities."

Krista was not overly impressed, but tried to make a polite request for his order. "Yes, Sir. I'm sure we can oblige with an excellent sample from our local waters. If you make a quick order we will have them cracked and served with mustard at the window to your left. You will be number 63."

Beasley stepped to the counter to explain with a drawl, "It's been a while since I've been here. We'll take 4 apiece and a couple of beers. My aide will buy, won't you Arnold? Looks like you have a profitable business!"

Krista smiled, "We work hard to supply our customers. I'll put that on your credit card if you like. Take your choice of a table in the sun or shade. Perhaps my friend and I will join you for a conversation about life on our boats."

Ten minutes later Krista was leading me by an elbow with

yours truly carrying two bowls of conch chowder to go sit with the Congressman. "Yes, perhaps you should know how we are coping with changes in fishing conditions in the Gulf. My companion, Professor Fairchild, is a visitor from Colorado who is studying the changing environment here."

Beasley was slightly curious. "These are changes for the better, I'm sure."

"Don't I wish!" Krista turned to me. "We've had some suspicions about why there aren't as many fish and stone crabs."

Beasley advised me, "Just more fishermen, don't you think?"

"Could be part of the problem." But then I added, "Basically, the fish food is different. Warmer water and increased acid changes things and sea life suffers. Of course, the pollution from the Glades spoils the hatchery conditions in the mangroves too."

"A slight price for economic progress, don't you think? Of course there are always environmental cycles too," Beasley insisted.

I tried to be agreeable, "Oh, there's the solar cycle, and volcanoes come and go. But this extra atmospheric CO_2 isn't going to go away for a very long time."

Beasley laughed. "Oh, come now! That's silly; we've had CO_2 forever—it makes the trees grow!" Arnold was sitting quietly with a puzzled scowl.

Krista complained, "Then why is our cycle of high and low tides getting higher and flooding our lawns? That didn't used to be a problem!"

I began to suspect that our Congressman and his aide had no idea of the climate problem. "But you must know of our problem here in Florida of sea level rise due to warmer water and melting glaciers; it's a little more than an inch every 10 years."

"Doesn't sound like much of a problem to me!" Beasley waved a hand. Arnold seemed to agree.

Krista disagreed. "But they think that fixing the sea level rise on the East Coast is going to use up all the cash we need to clean up the Everglades. And Washington isn't doing their part in the Everglades restoration either."

Beasley had the explanation. "Never enough money with all the wasteful spending in big government. We'll get that fixed some day!"

Clearly our Congressman hadn't a clue of the increasing cost of adaptation to climate change. I explained, "The folks with 4 ft mean sea level on Miami Beach seem to have an urgent problem of sea water in the streets as well as beach erosion. And global warming is going to make it more and more expensive!"

"All my professional advisors tell me that global warming is a fraud perpetrated by environmental extremists!" Beasley exclaimed. Arnold was laughing, "Miami Beach politics is pretty extreme too!"

Krista was upset. "All the scientists that we know about say that global warming and climate change are real. And we see it happening!" Then in a quiet aside to me, "He's pretty damn stupid!"

I thought it time to depart. My Florida friends need to elect a new Congressman!

It was just a week later that Beasley was back with an order for the Grouper Sandwich Special. As he joined me with a beer at a table in the shade, he explained, "Arnold has convinced me that our expense account won't cover more stone crabs. And he's wondering what happened to the poster we left for you. But we'd like to tell you what we discovered over in Miami Beach and the Lauderdale canal subdivisions."

I replied, "I heard that the wind blew your fancy poster into the river; it went out with the tide. And I'm sure the East Coast situation was obvious if you were there at high tide."

Beasley, lifting a finger towards Arnold, said, "But you need to know what Arnold learned from our engineering consultant in Washington about that problem."

Arnold was happy to be placed in the spotlight. "The Party's engineer from Harvard explained that all the high rise developments on the beach have produced a foot or so of subsidence along the shoreline. You need to add some more sand to your beaches."

"Oh, I wonder about that; we might just as likely see the entire peninsula sinking." I insisted, "There has to be sea level rise. We know the ocean is warmer and there has to be thermal expansion. And the fresh meltwater from Greenland has to go someplace."

Beasley argued, "My political colleagues say that a degree or so temperature change is uncertain and not a real concern. That's just bullshit."

Our local trash organizer had just earned his lunch and eased his eighty-some year old body onto a seat at the adjacent table. The contrast of his dilapidated straw hat and patched shirt and trousers with the Congressman's attire was a near joke. I had frequently visited with Jeremy about his borderline existence and gave him a friendly wave.

I renewed the discussion with Beasley with, "My background in History doesn't make me an expert on the physics, but the trend of temperature increase looks meaningful to me."

Arnold made the contribution, "Just supposed to tell you if you feel warm or cold."

Beasley made the token objection, "Doesn't mean much out there in the ocean."

Jeremy took this opportunity to join the conversation. "But them there water molercules kin feel the heat."

Arnold felt a need to clarify the subject. "I believe temperature measures the heat energy. Right?" And with my encouraging smile, he continued, "And some of the radical scientists claim that the Earth is absorbing too much energy." But with Beasley's frown, he added, "But that's just a theory."

I couldn't resist. "But isn't this a bit like your checking account? It's pretty fundamental: things have to balance. Heat coming in from the sun has to be balanced by heat out from the Earth."

Beasley waved a fork with French fry, "Sure, sunlight absorbed and reflected."

There was a bit of commotion inside as school had ended. Jessica accepted my invitation to join us, and Danny soon appeared with a pair of soft drinks. Jessica thanked Danny for the 7-Up and primed him with, "Heat radiation with visible sunlight in and Earth infrared going out. Right?"

Danny's reply was, "Sure. Scientists knew all about it a hundred years ago."

Beasley objected, "But these things need more research. Scientists don't agree on all the details."

I could see that Jeremy wanted us to understand that his experiences left little to be learned. I gave him a discrete wink to which he responded, "Us human's evolution made our eyes sensitive jest to the sun's very high temperature light. But I can still see the red light from the lower temperature coals in the fireplace, and I can still feel the infrared heat on my hands after the temperature drops a little more."Then looking directly towards our guests from Washington, "And you must know about the formulas that connect the total radiation to the temperature."

Arnold sat with open mouth. Beasley nodded with, "Lots of theories. Our experts aren't fooled by things you probably read in Rolling Stone".

Danny objected with, "Those are facts from intensity measurements and Absolute temperatures a hundred years ago." Then added, "And the quantum theory that fits helped us to invent all the modern things like computers and cell phones."

Beasley insisted, "But the so-called expert scientists with their climate models have to use big fancy computers that won't even give accurate weather forecasts. And my decisions in Washington have to be determined by information from folks like the Heartland Institute—far more reliable than from wannabe scientists and garbage collectors."

Jeremy was angry. "By damn, I was in uniform making weather measurements for the fly boys before them jokers was born!"

"And I believe the science facts that Jessica is using in her class to teach Danny and his friends are the most reliable up-to-date information that the Profs in Tallahassee have learned from NOAA and NASA." I gave Danny a reassuring smile and pat on the back. "And the Columbia and Princeton scientists use the most accurate science fundamentals; they need the fast computers to describe the details for the entire Earth."

Beasley became busy putting a few morsels aside for the gulls, then stated, "But our leaders in Congress are not convinced by backroom theories. Climate changes are just theoretical remarks by a few loud-mouthed scientists."

Jessica wasn't ready to sacrifice her science to be polite. "You just have to understand a few scientific facts. If you try to balance the Earth heat at the surface as you said earlier, you get the wrong answer by about 60 degrees. You have to include the atmospheric heat trapping by water molecules and a few others to get the correct temperature. And Earth is special; call it an Act of God or Intelligent Design, if you want. But if you do the correct mathematics, you find Mars is too cold and Venus is way too hot. Earth is just right for the evolution of humans and our plants and animals."

Jeremy spoke out with, "I sure don't want to go to Venus and can't afford the NASA trip to Mars. You folks damn well better take care of this ole planet for my next 20 years."

Beasley objected, "But my Congressional colleagues won't let you fiddle with the mathematics to claim that we have global warming."

Danny was serious. "This is the same science and mathematics that fit the observations a hundred years ago. But we've got maybe 10 times the number of people, and some of the numbers, especially for greenhouse gases, don't give a balanced climate anymore. And all the science people say that we can't go back to our old climate."

Arnold was shaking his head. "We have lots of water and no way can we change the amount. There's the same old cycle of rain and evaporation."

"And this talk about CO_2 is just a scare tactic." Beasley was a bit arrogant. "We can always use more to make the corn and wheat grow."

I remembered Dr. Alley's story of the control knob. "A little more atmospheric CO_2 from burning coal and a slight boost in temperature means more evaporation from the oceans and a lot more atmospheric water vapor greenhouse effect." And I remembered the scary thing. "Sure, the water vapor cycle is only about 10 days. But the CO_2 cycles in and out of the atmosphere are centuries long. The extra CO_2 that we put into the air from burning coal and oil today will trap additional heat for hundreds of years. Danny will not see today's climate for the rest of his life."

Beasley was defensive. "Trying to shut off the coal and make enough solar panels and wind turbines will ruin our economy and spoil things for the people who live today. We just have to wait for things to get better."

As Danny stood to go play soccer, he whispered to Jeremy. "Who were the stupid people who voted for him! I'm sure you know better, and make sure your bingo friends know how to vote!"

My Climate Corps contacts occasionally e-mailed me to make certain that I was up to date on the climate science. They were familiar with the Orbatz website discussions of course, but they had also attended a Gold Coast symposium on adaptations to sea level rise. The symposium was inspired by several significant storm surge beach erosion events and frequent residential inundations from the long ocean fetch caused by large storms far out in the Atlantic. This led to identification of various weak areas in the beach dunes for future strengthening efforts with extra sand. There had also been a gradual increase in the salt content of the fresh water wells serving the coastal area. There was considerable saline fluctuation, especially in the Biscayne aquifer, from seasonal rainfall. Some efforts to fix this had involved pumping summer-fall floodwater into a lower aquifer as emergency storage. This water quality was necessarily improved through use of an increasing number of desalination operations. The ultimate goal of the meeting was to organize a need for future local voter approval of tax or bond proposals for infrastructure improvements. Considerable skepticism was voiced about its possible success; only K-12 education had a lower priority. Sentiment seemed to be: if it ain't broke, don't fix it. Besides, it was argued, if we get a bad storm sometime in the future, FEMA is supposed to take care of it. But the knowledgeable folks in Washington know that FEMA will protect its budget by expecting that Florida locals will have enough resources to fix their own problem.

My young Climate Corps friends were dismayed that there was no discussion of the real cause of sea level rise, climate change. There was no mention of energy conservation or projects for renewable energy. There were no efforts for political action to address the increased greenhouse gas emissions; any attempts to address the cause were viewed with antagonism by the establishment. The symposium participants were apparently led to believe that adaptation activities were the most that could be politically supported.

Alice

It soon became apparent that Nature would quickly take the lead in the east coast problems. Tropical Storm Alice was following the Gulf Stream out of the Florida Straits. There was some hope that the storm would move out into the Atlantic to become someone else's problem. However, the track was destined to move parallel to the coast; the winds increased and there was the suggestion of an eye in satellite pictures. All business and construction activity abruptly ceased and residents swarmed the supermarkets for batteries, ice, and bottled water. High tide in early evening with the onshore wind brought brackish water into the residential canals and heavy rain topped the surge onto the lawns. Alice was upgraded to a Category I hurricane. While the eyewall winds remained just offshore, frequent gusts toppled power transformers and fallen power lines ceased to deliver electricity. Morning found the storm lingering over the Gulf Stream and the low-pressure center wandered onto the beach at Ft. Lauderdale with 3 inches of rain every hour. The downpour did not cease; by day's end all highways and streets were impassable with several feet of water.

In Everglades City we found ourselves on the fringe of the storm with frequent thundershowers moving out of the Glades. The following day we began to get TV coverage of the east coast situation from mobile units. The morning tide along with the continuing rain had inundated businesses and homes from Palm Beach to Miami. The beach dunes had been breached in numerous locations and the Intracoastal was virtually continuous from Federal Highway to the Atlantic. The National Guard had begun to transport fuel to hospital emergency generators and bottled water to Red Cross shelters. Some of our Climate Corps people were patrolling the streets in kayaks for emergency rescues.

It was nearly a week later when the flood began to recede. Electric power was iffy; crews found flooded streets and downed power lines making the situation treacherous. Pumps were slow to operate in emptying homes and businesses. Older citizens had experienced such nuisances at various times in the past but this was more extreme. Some members of the New Generation Climate Corps were concerned that these difficulties promised to become a way of life for their future. They became inspired to mobilize for a protest march against officials for ignoring the scientists' warning that the increases in sea level rise were almost certainly due to human caused climate change. They discovered the Facebook network very effective in attracting hundreds of the younger generation for a barefoot march down flooded Federal Highway from Boca Raton to Ft. Lauderdale. There were plans to entice visitors from surrounding states to expand the demonstration to block traffic from Palm Beach to Miami. Needless to say, this gathering of young people degenerated into a party atmosphere. Not a few were completely unaware of the scientific facts that were the excuse for this exuberant behavior.

The Monday morning edition of the Palm Beach Post headlined this fiasco with "Spring Weekend Returns With Celebration of Nature's Excess". I was amused but wondered how soon the establishment would become fed up with the activities. I was happy to find the conch chowder supply at the fish market was healthy and had an active discussion with Krista and eventually with John and Luisa about the East Coast ruckus. John was clearly upset, "The wealthy residents over there are going to find the protests to be a real nuisance. They've had heavy weather over there before and will expect the water to recede in a few days. They can afford to put up with the extra expense so they can enjoy normal warm sunshine again. Their only concern is the smelly mold that took over when the power for AC was off. And the politicians they elected have claimed they are back in control; not to worry!"

Then a few days later I saw the Orbatz website with a new message:

orbatzintheeverglades.com

VI. Protest

Our younger generation is fully justified in expecting their elders to respond with political action to control the global warming that is causing the sea level rise and weather extremes. In contrast to their elders, they know that these events are caused by the reliance on fossil fuel generation of power. In the near future the residents may very well experience a Florida episode of the Hurricane Sandy type. Then the East Coast demonstrations could threaten to become the societal revolution that is long overdue. The failure of the powers that be to understand and respect the scientific basis for this disrupted climate

may simply set the stage for an escalation of the pro-tests to a violent level against the inaction of their elders.

I suggest that we abandon hope for those wealthy in control on the East Coast who selfishly refuse to correct their environmental policies. Our Climate Corps has demonstrated a positive correction to power generation in the support of renewable energy from solar and wind. Their constructive movement is expanding. But the climate science is not generally available without serious reading and it seems that members of the public, including this new generation, have lost the habit of such activity. Members of the Corps are making constructive use of the social media to communicate the scientific details, but this movement cannot hope to bring about a major nationwide elimination of fossil fuel generation of power. Still, many financial institutions have begun to recognize the need to divest from fossil fuels and support the renewables activated by our New Generation Climate Corps.

Get serious, young folks, and pay attention, oldsters!

I must belatedly confess to those denial comments attributed to Zorbat, Torbaz, Bortaz, and Borzat. You have probably noticed the permutations on my name; they were designed to stir up attention and controversy.

Professor Orbatz

The Program

A few days later I checked the Dell for an internet update on the rest of the world; I was slightly surprised by a Got Mail from John.

To Priusman

I just had a last minute notice from our political has-beens. They predict favorable weather at the chickee for the weekend and thought it might be good to get a progress report from our Climate Corps, so bring Jessica with whatever info she has. And we have a proposal for funding from our Climate Corps in the Keys that needs your expert advice. Weather and bug prediction suggest you might want to do a sleepover after the usual barbeque, so get Krista to come equipped for whatever. Some strings are attached: BYOB and dessert, key lime pie preferred; there will be barbequed Kingfish and hearts of palm salad.

John.

Glades II

When we arrived at the chickee via Jasper's airboat we found a delegation from Key West that had enjoyed Friday night airboat transport and Glades sleeping accommodations.

The Judge excused himself with the suggestion, "Please introduce yourselves; I'm too absent minded to get things straight." We managed that without disaster. The husky pair from the Conch Republic answered to Walter and Benjamin, "Walt and Ben, if you please."

The Judge suggested, "Apparently we have moved beyond discussions about lifestyles to attention to the environment. It is a common problem independent of religion or whatever." After a quick response to the chuckles, he continued in a more serious vein. "My former environmental friends back in Palm Beach take pride in supporting activities at the Loxahatchee National Refuge. But there was no hint of the need for renewable energy at the new Visitor Center. And there has been no mention of a solar farm for that strip of private land just east of the Refuge. Florida Electric might actually be convinced to support that to provide power to that huge residential development in Boynton Beach. But unfortunately the almighty dollar dominated Florida Electric's thinking when they turned down the wind farm out in the Glades in favor of cheaper natural gas. They should get educated about the ultimate need for renewables with gas only as a backup. Of course they get no feedback from the public; there was the annual keynote lecture at Loxahatchee by a scientist who explained the scientific details and recommended immediate consideration of solar energy and a need for leadership in ending the reliance on fossil fuels, but further public discussions have not mentioned the subject."

This was clearly no surprise to the group and we settled down for a bit of socializing. Ben explained that he and Walt had been classmates at Oberlin, and after enduring several cold and snowy winters in Ohio, had hitchhiked to Key West for Spring Break. "A pair of ladies on Duval St. thought that Oberlin graduates would improve the cultural atmosphere of their art museum/shop, and our history background gave us a shot at a role in the Hemingway and Truman tours. It looked more interesting and appealing than being unemployed in Brooklyn, so we've settled in."

The Overseas Highway and Key West had always been on my travel itinerary. I had even begged Danny to help me search the internet for tourist attractions in Key West. There were turtle and aquarium exhibits as expected, but also tours of houses that were reputed to have been residences of Audubon and Hemingway, and considerable publicity about the more recent exploits of Mel Fisher, an explorer of underwater ship wrecks. His successful 1985 discovery of the cargo treasure of the Spanish ship Atocha was given considerable attention on the website for its display in his Maritime Museum.

I learned from the website that he had also stumbled on the wreck of an English slave ship, the Henrietta Marie. Some crewman cargo was on display, but the ship was on tour. And I was surprised to find considerable history of that slave trade.

Ships from England would take a load of slaves from Africa to Cuba for work on sugar plantations, then return to England. But after the Civil War, the U.S. Navy set up a blockade and captured three of those ships. They brought the slaves to a compound in Key West where there is now a gravesite memorial. After a few years the U.S. government shipped the surviving slaves to a final home in Liberia.

So Danny and I learned a lot about the history of Key West. But I had continued to procrastinate about departing Everglades City and the personal attractions at Island Seafood. I had often wondered about Key West, "Being one of the few really historic cities in Florida makes it unique. But is that enough to support the residents?"

Walt answered, "We've always been a tourist destination with Hemingway's tavern, Truman's Little White House, deep sea fishing, and the turtle and aquarium exhibits, not to mention the pervasive party atmosphere and visits by cruise ships. The cultural attractions of the Hemingway House and the Aububon House are also standard tourist traps. The Maritime Museum that you described is relatively new. But we are becoming more isolated by sea level rise. It has become necessary for Key West residents and tourists alike to cope with flooding in the streets at the full moon. The Overseas is flooded in spots and traffic only works for a few hours a day. The locals plan accordingly but the tourists find themselves stymied with a moon-dependent schedule."

Ben added, "I'm afraid the future of Key West as a tourist destination will be severely damaged. The Overseas Highway will be closed much of the time. The cruise ships won't stop if our streets are inconveniently flooded. We may actually be without power for long periods if any kind of storm damages the lines and repairs are delayed by high tides on the highway. I can imagine the loss of business will close many of our shops, and the power company may very well decide to close down altogether. We could be dependent on diesel generators, like the Dry Tortugas."

Jessica noted, "Continuing sea level rise is pretty much a sure thing with State and Federal governments refusing to deal with increasing greenhouse gas emissions. The highway journey down the Keys and around the city streets is going to be a sloshy mess. So how will you manage? Will Duval St. be sufficient to attract wealthy winter residents?"

Walt replied, "Actually, I understand that the Tortugas is transitioning from diesel to solar. So our plan is to abandon the undependable power company's monopoly and go for a complete free solar system, something like you have in Everglades City. Tourists will always come, but we will have to tighten our belts. Can you help us?"

The Judge suggested, "If you were truly a separate Conch Republic with an independent budget we might be able to cooperate on a long term project. I understand there are some battery storage developments that could get you completely on solar."

The Senator queried, "So how can we make it happen?"

Walt replied, "We've been bootlegging time during the gaps of customer visits to our Hemingway and Audubon tours to make detailed plans. We were hoping to support our tourist facilities with overhead solar panels on all our east-west and waterfront streets. Residential areas are already taking steps to get rooftop systems. And we could be more energy efficient:

you may know that the Hemingway House has never needed air conditioning. Most of our modern buildings would quickly sprout a layer of mildew, but we could probably give that some scrutiny. And we could switch out all the incandescents to CFLs and LEDs. We know that would pay off if we could just make the initial investment."

Ben added, "We might get the tourists back if we could just deal with street flooding. We're working with the navy shops to help us move to high clearance electric buses for local traffic."

Our atmosphere was very quiet except for a distant rumble of thunder. The Senator stood to announce, "Well, I have some spare cash and we can work with you on an initial shipment of solar panels. If the Chinese cooperate with my investment, you can expect a shipment of panels and hardware in a week or so. You will need to do the hands-on work of installation." The Senator smiled, sipped at his wine, and looked about for comments. "Go for it!!"

Jessica volunteered, "You need our Climate Corps. If you can furnish the solar hardware and spring for our expenses while we are there, I suspect that my Climate Corps folks could take a long holiday in the sun to help you. Perhaps you could actually become an independent Conch Republic, our 51st state. And we could work on some way to get you more energy efficient."

As we were returning to what passes for Florida civilization, Jessica gave me a nudge and asked, "Like to see my new posts from followers on Facebook?"

"Oh yes! Some of those followers have been giving some careful thought to the climate!"

When the Prius delivered Jessica to her small house, she opened her laptop to the posts.

Miriam, at Sun-Sentinel

I followed Billy's instructions to visit that Everglades site out west of the campground on highway 27. Nothing there but alligators and sawgrass; that's Orbatz' research?

Miccosukee Billy

Ah, but we have to be patient with that very elusive professor, don't you know! There is a rumor that he has migrated to 25°12'47.22"N/80°31'7.46"W.

James, Engineering student in the Climate Corps

Zachary's story a while back of the Earth's radiation transfer was incomplete. About half way up in the troposphere, our lower atmosphere where weather happens, the greenhouse gas densities are not great enough to continue to efficiently absorb that radiation. So the radiation can escape to space. In fact, that is the radiation surface at that temperature of 255K that my New Generation friends in Key West calculated. And the escaping water vapor radiation at 6 microns is what we detect from a satellite to produce the TV pictures of water vapor trapped below the cold boundary at the tropopause.

As I returned her laptop after a careful study, Jessica asked, "So Prof, when are you going to join the rest of the world in communicating on Facebook?"

"Jessica, you must realize I'm in that generation of old fogies that are stuck with the idea that you need to be able to look a person in the eye to get the full meaning of a conversation. And I suspect that my retirement would be more relaxing without a continual electronic probe of what I am doing, when I am doing it, and with whom I might choose to do it."

I really didn't want to expose my slow understanding of such a procedure. My solution was a consultation with Danny. In just one hour after Danny was out of school he had me enrolled. All my personal interests, education, age-upper middle, and silly picture in shorts and tee shirt. And I got an immediate hit from a lady high school teacher in Driggs, Idaho, who wondered if I would drop by on my way to Yellowstone National Park—if I was Mormon.

So it was just a day later that I arrived at Krista's shop as she was enlightening John about my new Facebook abilities. I thought to make an effective change of subject, so I suggested to John, "Do you suppose that it's time to formalize the environmental movement legally with this Nature's Trust? Think we should talk to the Judge about it?"

"Yes, he would have some excellent opinions. But I'm

afraid the judicial is too much under political control just now."

Jessica overheard some of this as she arrived with her lunch. She paused with her sandwich to ask me, "Prof, do you think we might have another top level meeting with the Judge and Senator in the Glades? My Climate Corps construction team is having an uphill battle getting on-the-ground cooperation to continue renewable energy projects. We're finding that many of our generation need convincing of the magnitude of the climate problem. They are content to sit back and twiddle their thumbs with business as usual; they assume that the government will fix it if necessary. We need a schedule." John was nodding agreement.

Glades III Policy Shift

A week later the Prius convoy was on the way to Forty-Mile Bend to meet with a pair of Climate Corps officers from the east. Jasper and a friend were ready with the airboat and swamp buggy to ferry a crew of nine like-minded folks to the chickee.

On our arrival, the Judge explained that his Miccosukee friends would arrive later with food for all. As we settled in, Jessica volunteered to bring us up to date on the Climate Corps activities. "As you know, the local power people have cooperated with the politicians to maintain a monopoly on selling electricity in South Florida. And their profit line depends on continuing to burn coal from Colombia and avoiding the transition to renewable energy. But between the Orbatz website and our Climate Corps efforts, some of the major businesses have begun to achieve zero carbon emissions. They are working with us to install solar panels for independent grid-connected solar power in their shopping areas. And some are anticipating an increase in the numbers of electric cars and are following Marco's example of incorporating free solar energy as an attraction in their mall parking."

"But we've become aware that the fossil fuel people have done a real job on stalling the awareness of climate change. Our generation has been left ignorant of the science by public schools and universities. The school boards and faculties of our elders have felt they were too busy with the fossil fuel business as usual to set the record straight on the real environmental danger and our education in that area has been sorely neglected. We find little welcome at the frontier of our renewable energy projects. So now we've begun to reorganize our efforts for informal science lessons on Facebook."

Krista added, "Yes, I've noticed that Danny and his friends are spending a lot of time on that; it's actually competing with advice for scoring in sexual activities!"

We were hoping for more details, but the Judge wondered, "I have the impression that these social networks are international. We need to make this a long-range goal. Other countries might follow our lead in reducing emissions, but better to get the new generation in China and India and the developing countries on board to move things along."

I thought to lighten up the atmosphere. "Maybe we will have an influx of environmental fairies to capture those CO_2 molecules." That produced a few giggles, but dropped like a lead balloon.

John added a complication, "They have a closely related problem that has to be acknowledged. Although it's an established fact that the industrialized countries of the West are primarily responsible for the present buildup of greenhouse gases, the population explosion in the developing countries following the biological laws of multiplication makes this an equally nasty problem. If they were to develop a technology capable of the same per capita greenhouse gas emission as we in the U.S. produce, we would have a tipping point of an even greater dimension. The problems are clearly related. The control of population is at least as complicated as controlling the use of fossil fuel and there is at present only slight indication of progress. Still, the minimum time for population control is one human generation, say about 50 years. On the other hand, the carbon cycles are long and the oceans won't cool for something like a thousand years. So if the environmental danger were given the same attention as a wartime emergency in the industrial countries, the climate might be in sufficient control so that the religious fanatics in the developing countries will finally become aware of the pitfalls of the population explosion. But the present apathy leading to a disastrous climate change on the planet may not give civilization a second chance at population control."

I began to identify these thoughts as an Orbatz lecture. John continued, "We need to quickly demonstrate the relatively simple physical control of the climate with renewable energy sources before the global warming gets completely out of hand. Then the developing nations would have the opportunity to attend to their food and shelter problems and face the problem of population explosion. Of course humans may still fail to address population control. Then human civilizations might settle for a cruel combination of immigration control by nations favored with food production and continued starvation for others. Civilization need not completely collapse even then; portions of the planet would still be habitable."

The Judge added, "Which brings us to another matter that should be mentioned. My good friend Billy, the Miccosukee, has been baiting a media person named Helen—she has never had good things to say about the tribe—about the location of our good friend, Orbatz. According to Billy, Orbatz' secret location was identified by specific GPS coordinates someplace in the remote eastern Glades. And sure 'nuff, Helen and others in helicopters showed up promptly to get pictures and interviews and discovered they had found an alligator in the sawgrass. But Billy's most recent GPS coordinates were actually for an abandoned camp occasionally used by deer hunters. Recently Billy learned that a helicopter, without standard identification, was observed near there. When he made a brief excursion out there, he discovered the shack had sustained a few dozen bullet holes. That kind of attention is rather at odds with an interview and pictures." The Judge paused, then with a sidelong glance at John he remarked, "Evidently our esteemed mentor Professor Orbatz has an antagonist out there suffering from renewed offense at Orbatz' activism about climate change on his website." John and the Judge maintained a long mutual stare.

Luisa's restraining hand on John's shoulder was accompanied by an expression of concern. But with a long sigh, John chuckled, "So Orbatz in the Everglades continues to be elusive." Then his smile vanished and he said, "And there continues to be a certain class of Florida citizen who discovers that logic and money won't always accomplish what he wants, so he resorts to guns and bullets. Evidently our efforts to begin correction of energy and transport dependent on fossil fuel production have gone beyond the stubborn intransigence of most of our citizens and have now stirred up some violent opposition."

John stared out the door at the wind-blown cabbage palm. "As Rodney used to say, "I get no respect". That could be the lament of Orbatz when he talks about the Greenhouse Effect on his website. The laws of natural science have apparently never been carefully studied by the climate change deniers or by the majority of the voters in this state. Our public schools and universities give token attention to science literacy and the students make little distinction between nature's laws and the rules of behavior on city streets. We seem to be following the philosophy of the Rex Stout mystery stories of the sixties. Stout's hero, Nero Wolfe, once said that scientists should keep their findings strictly to themselves; by spilling it they just complicate things for other people. Of course everyone appreciates the force of gravity in everyday life and accepts the universal law of gravitation. But the doubted consequences of the greenhouse effect are equally observable and the basic theory has been known for a hundred years."

Then after a moment of thought, "And there's a fundamental difference between the invariant science of the universe and the human constructs of economics and governments. You have no doubt about the result if you fall off the roof of your house, and so you behave accordingly. The result of increasing the concentrations of greenhouse gases in the atmosphere is as certain as gravity's result in the roof incident. The consequences are potentially as disastrous as war and equally applicable to the poor and to the rich polluters. The similarity of Joe Blow's and his neighbor's greed for cheap energy to the Tragedy of the Commons is poorly recognized. The notion of making a sacrifice for the common good doesn't cut it! There is little recognition of the cause of human greed leading to a failure of intelligent responsibility. The likely result is the eventual disaster to all of human civilization. We have the common adversary of climate change driven by the fossil fuel enhancement of the greenhouse effect in the natural laws of the universe."

"But this must not diminish our local dedication to using

our intelligence to do what's right about our planet home. Your Professor Orbatz has been known to say it like it is. I believe the expression is "A man's got to do what a man's got to do!" But when the skin divers find his granite memorial, they will probably read "I TOLD YOU SO!" Of course Orbatz has had some pleasant distractions lately." There was a quick loving glance at Luisa.

The room was deeply quiet; I could feel the atmosphere of respectful understanding. The spirit of Orbatz was among us! In the quiet interval I cautiously suggested, "I believe we can continue to adopt the spirit of Orbatz' dedication without endangering his lifestyle. And our support on Facebook and Twitter can also proceed without making groups or individuals targets for violence. I think we can maintain a low profile in the necessary office work at the Senator's condo. And another bill or two on the 40-mile bar would probably ensure Jasper's increased caution. This chickee doesn't need a helicopter visit, especially if we are having a party."

As if to agree, there was an overhead grumble followed by a lightning bolt with a prompt thunderclap. This was the prelude to a sudden downpour that required some slight maneuvers to avoid leaks in the chickee thatch. The deluge ended as abruptly as it had started and Jessica indicated a desire to contribute. "Many of the science communications to the public take the form of the results of computer programs. I wonder if that isn't a mistake. E. O. Wilson, the famous Harvard sociobiologist and the world's greatest expert on ants, has said that people may respect scientific writing, but they read novels. So he wrote one. I also hear that professional science communicators have advocated that readers would pay more attention to a story approach, so we are attempting to do exactly that in some of our Facebook communications."

This sounded like it might work for my University students. I wondered though, "You know, our neighbors on the East Coast who are currently upset about a bit of salt in their drinking water may not be into this Facebook thing. They seem to be ignorant of any predictions of further climate change and are going to find themselves with an awful disaster far beyond anything they are presently fussing about." I paused for a new thought. "I wonder if the concept of future events beyond a five day weather forecast is even in their genes!"

In the brief lull in conversation, the Senator explained, "I made a brief reference to my lady friend in Boca who endeavors to keep me a bit more socially active than I could manage on my own. She is the widow of a big box manager back in Ohio, so she is naturally in some demand for dinner engagements, bridge parties and charitable activities. As her escort, my former political activity is conveniently overlooked. This has given me some rather clear insight into the philosophy of those influential individuals of my generation about environmental matters. They have been exposed to enough of the climate change undercurrent to form a fairly firm policy of behavior. Their economic outlook and conservative stance on any change forms the basis for thinking of such problems as a nuisance. Any moral stance on a responsibility for their surroundings or the next generation is completely absent. Adaptation measures to ensure their ability to obtain household services and attend the next social function are, of course, a necessity. There will be no movement to a government solution with that sort of voter attitude."

As our group concentrated for a few minutes on their chips, I tried to organize my thoughts. I was thinking of a major shift in emphasis. "The Climate Corps work on the ground for construction of solar and wind facilities should continue, of course. And we need an educated new generation to expand this work. And finally, we must convince our leaders to adopt this change nationwide. It is futile to expect climate deniers and their elderly disciples to study the Orbatz website and use the information to become politically active. Instead, let us concentrate on communicating with the new generation who will soon vote. I wonder if more communication on the social networks might identify and replace the climate change deniers in our government. Then with more constructive leadership our grassroots projects for renewable energy might be more successful."

The Judge commented, "I hate to admit to a serious political thought. Replacing that do-nothing Congress with some intelligent people might actually work!" Then, sitting with a frown, "But we'll need the votes of this old do-nothing generation as well. That's an entirely different campaign level. They only understand high society affairs and economic growth. So that will be a very uphill project. The present establishment has things locked up; the media as well as Florida government employees are forbidden to even mention the words global warming or climate change. I wonder if there might be some related project that would reopen the subject."

"You know," interrupted the Senator. "My lady friend in Boca did mention hearing about a Palm Beach widow lady fixed with too much old money who was trying to think of some activity that would be a memorial to her late husband.

He left a Tesla toy parked in their garage; she wonders if it might be a good time to expand the electric car business for folks who are flush with cash. The BMW and Porsche people are ready to compete with Tesla, and that suggests a need for clean electricity from solar. Tesla already has charging stations at major Florida hotels around the state and has plans for stations along the Interstates. I believe our Climate Corps could have discussions with the electric car companies to equip the stations with the necessary solar panels and contract with our Corps members for the installation. This will not only eliminate the need for liquid fossil fuel but will also bypass the grid monopoly."

I stood and clapped hands, "Bravo! The Rod and Gun Club can get a Tesla charging station in their parking lot and we can have lots of publicity for Everglades City renewables. Luisa can trade in her old Toyota."

Krista spoke up, "Everglades City already has the solar; Island Seafood has the space for a Leaf charging station and whatever."

John was eyeing Luisa, "Do you suppose it's time for Orbatz to get out of the sawgrass?"

"Think on it!" from the Judge.

John stood and finished his beer, then announced, "If there is no more serious business, I suggest we move to the air boat before the next shower arrives."

On our return to the Trail, I followed through and cautioned Jasper about the need for increased vigilance regarding the safety of Orbatz and the Everglades chickee. He replied,

"Funny you mention it! Had some family thoughts over break-fast about the damage of our Glades from ig'orant city folks shootin' our birds and gators, and startin' fires in the sawgrass. Daughter Cindy came up with a project to warn them off. She did some photoshopping with a Miccosukee dressed like a bloodthirsty savage holding a shoulder-fired surface-to-air missile. Another with that tourist copter crash on the beach at Lauderdale—moved it out to the Glades. And another view of my buddy Sam's wreck of his airboat—we could make up a story of the fate of the tourists as food for the gators. I thought to give these to Billy to wave in front of that gullible Helen newsperson. Might even suggest she look where the pilots flew that L-1011 into the sawgrass—must still be a few frag-ments out there. And cu'd give the chickee a little backcountry look—I have an old flatbottom skiff that we could anchor near there—might hang a few gator skins alongside. Anyways, we'll keep our cards close to our chest at the 40-Mile bar."

Tesla I Introduction

A week later, Jessica had her minions installing a Leaf charging station at the Island Seafood parking lot. They were all dressed in green work clothes, "Just in case." I thought that a bit much. But Krista argued that it might actually improve business. I sat by the water with my grouper basket and wondered: I thought John might have some insight about that. I figured he would be about due for fish shopping; sure 'nuff, heard the bike tires in the parking lot—but just a bit too noisy. Best check on that.

I nearly dropped my lunch at the sight of the gleaming red sports car sitting in the middle of the parking lot. That had to be a Tesla!! Luisa, in a neat chauffeur uniform, stepped smartly away from driver's side. A familiar Climate Corps youth in matching chauffeur's uniform moved from the passenger side to open the rear door for an impressive personage in black cap and gown. The academic sporting the neat mustache and goatee brandished a cane as he approached the fish market entrance. His attendant followed to relieve his charge of cap and gown to reveal a professorial figure with purple vest and bow tie and standard tan corduroy jacket complete with leather elbow patches. Jessica stepped to his side to make the introduction. "Our New Generation Climate Corps is proud to introduce Professor John Orbatz to discuss the opportunity for modern electric vehicle transportation in this era of rapid climate change."

"Good day my fellow Floridians. There are more than seven billion humans on planet Earth. Only the insects outnumber us. Humans have the basic intelligence to adapt to the geographic and variable extremes of temperature that the planet has to offer. Nature is no longer our independent companion. Our activities in moving about, collecting food and using our natural resources have made us an integral part of the planet's ecosystem."

The Professor's voice was very familiar; my neighbors were chuckling and I heard, "Give 'em Hell, John!" He gave us a sly smile. I had no problem with that, but I had a further thought. Perhaps John really was that elusive professor, as I had begun to suspect.

He continued, "Our climate is going to follow Nature's laws involving the Atmospheric Greenhouse Effect. We have done a not-so-very-smart thing in knowingly increasing the greenhouse gas concentrations and have upset our planet's ability to maintain a stable climate. The choice isn't 'to believe or not to believe'. We have shown the human-caused increase of trace greenhouse gases like CO_2 functions as a control knob on thermal infrared trapping by an immense blanket of water vapor to produce global warming and subsequent climate change irreversible on our family's time scale."

"But with our technologic advances in solar and wind energy we can have the advantage of fossil free automobile propulsion. The Tesla car, named for a pioneer in electricity, is the ultimate in luxury travel. I trust you will enjoy your future in this 21st Century Climate."

"And now my youthful Climate Corps disciples will be happy to answer any questions about the science of global warming and climate change that we are now experiencing".

My Everglades City neighbors paused only briefly for "Hear! Hear!" and I joined them in active applause. He gave a brief wave of cane and turned majestically to carefully step aboard the Tesla. The vehicle quietly returned to the street to be escorted away by several husky Cuban attendants; I suspected they were distant relatives of Luisa.

Krista joined me from the kitchen to exclaim, "John makes an excellent professor." We exchanged a mutual stare; she stopped abruptly with open mouth and with an understanding smile, "And I do believe he's the real thing!"

PART IV LEADERSHIP

Carlos

I was about to wander down to the Market for a snack and a visit with Krista when my cell phone woke from a long nap to complain that someone wanted to bend my ear. The call was from a 303 number; that could be any of a few hundred former colleagues. I answered and heard, "Hello, Professor Fairchild, this is Carlos Martinez calling. I was a student in your class many years ago, and am now a resident of the Community up in the Colorado mountains west of our university. If you have a minute, I'll explain this interruption of your day in the Florida sun."

"Oh yes. I believe you were student body president. What's up?"

"Actually I'm visiting Sanibel, attending a meeting with the New Generation Climate Corps next week. I understand from Chris Baldwin, an assistant to Prof Mandryka, that you are associated with that group in Everglades City. Jessica Murphy, president of your local group, got wind of our Community workshop activities and convinced us that we should concentrate on climate change mitigation work. With her advice, we now have a Climate Corps. Our new Chapter plans to cooperate with the Community for a workshop and renewable energy projects in the mountains. So now I'm checking on your successes to see how we should start. I wonder if I might come down to talk with you about these New Generation activities."

ALEX COOK

A few days later I was sitting with John beside the Barron River introducing Carlos to conch chowder. We had finished the history of our meetings in the Glades and the Corps activities from Marco Island to Key West. I had a question for Carlos.

"Our Climate Corps workers are experiencing some apathy to their expansion of solar and wind energy. Many of the other young people they meet have no awareness of climate change, or have been brainwashed by the denier propaganda. The school boards for the public schools have generally refused to make it part of the curriculum. Have you experienced that?"

"There does seem to be considerable ignorance and apathy out there. Professor Mandryka has been working to establish a required general education course in climate change science at Golden West. It's moving slowly, however, and many of our undergrads have no exposure to the greenhouse effect science and the way the global warming by CO_2 is driving other climate changes. They know about the move towards wind and solar energy and assume it's just a reaction to the dangers of nuclear power. And of course the fossil fuel industry is happy with that distraction."

Carlos continued, "But in my research about other university's programs I stumbled on a Doctor of Education thesis. The title was "Cycles of Climate Change". The abstract indicated that the present brief natural cycle should be acknowledged in the teacher preparation for course work on climate adaptation in K-12 and college undergraduate work. There was little mention of the reality of the human increase of the centuries long lifetime of CO_2 from burning of fossil fuels." He added, "With neglected science like this, who needs the fossil fuel propaganda?"

John shook his head with, "I guess the Orbatz website isn't working! But how was the conference?"

"Well, the opening address was a lengthy detailed explanation of the science of the atmospheric greenhouse effect by Sam Clark of your New Generation Climate Corps. It was a complete and I thought very convincing explanation of human-caused climate change. But his offer of an open discussion was ignored and swamped by a series of lengthy shallow remarks about natural cycles and volcanic eruptions. I couldn't find anything else constructive on the agenda so I decided to go sightseeing."

I was disappointed. "Ouch! That's very discouraging. But, at least Sanibel has some special sights."

Carlos continued, "Well, I started with a walk on the beach, but my beach wanderings were unproductive. Evidently you need to patrol the low tide level immediately after a storm to beat the little old ladies in tennis shoes to any new shells. So the hotel clerk sent me over to the Ding Darling National Wildlife Refuge for the afternoon. The name didn't sound promising, but I learned that Darling originated the idea of a duck stamp to preserve habitat for waterfowl. I suspect he was a duck hunter when he wasn't drawing cartoons for some Iowa newspaper. And the refuge turned out to be a collection of mangrove islands separated by large areas of shallow brackish water. Obviously not ideal for residential development, so they give it to the birds. I found that the birds and their senior citizen admirers were very happy with the arrangement. I learned from an aggressive visitor sporting a Notre Dame sweatshirt that the big white birds sitting on the water with the very bulky bills were swans; a local couple found this to be terribly amusing. There was a flock of small birds with reddish brown feathers that were actively searching under the waterline shells for food; I thought they should be called turnstones and the local couple surprisingly agreed! The large black logs in the next pond turned out to be alligators. Some long legged, long billed white birds were sharing the muddy water. It looked like risky cohabitation to me!"

We smiled our agreement and Carlos continued, "A grumbling black cloud connected to the water with jagged lightning flashes convinced me to tour the refuge museum. I promptly learned more about the Florida environment and weather than I ever thought I wanted to know. But I was unable to find any mention of climate change. Looks like Florida folks are just going to sit back and let their environment go down the tube!"

"Our Colorado voters are more concerned about the environment and less dominated by the political-utilities control that you have here in Florida. But we still get a lot of fossil fuel propaganda. We have been inspired by the efforts of Professor Mary Wood from Oregon to initiate a legal challenge to protect what she calls Nature's Trust. We have formed a cell with this emphasis that can eventually expand to State, Federal, and International activity."

Jessica Murphy arrived just as we gave up on the world's problems and sat back to enjoy our after lunch beer. As she began to work on her grouper sandwich, I moved to introduce her to Carlos. Jessica interrupted, "We met briefly at Sanibel.

We've already agreed that we need to formalize the efforts of the Climate Corps with the Community network in the mountains."

Carlos added, "And the Sanibel program emphasized that there's work to be done. I wonder if I might join in your next Glades meeting; our mountain Community might be helpful."

I agreed. "Yes, I believe your efforts in education and communication might be very helpful. We should probably start to formulate a long-term plan. And you should be familiar with the support of the Judge, the Senator, and Orbatz.

Glades IV Workshop

Two days later the Prius convoy was on the way to Forty-mile Bend. Carlos had offered to shop for some Mexican food for snacks. We added a supply of beverages that the saloon was happy to furnish. As we settled in at the chickee for drinks and chips, I introduced our newcomer from Colorado. "Carlos is a former student from my university. He has been active in environmental issues at a place called The Community in the Rockies. He came down to Sanibel for the climate meeting and was disappointed, so we wondered if he could contribute in some way with the New Generation Climate Corps."

"Yes! The Community! I have heard a few things about your workshops. Good to have you on board!" The Judge extended a welcoming hand, "But you're going to have to stretch a bit to fill the footsteps of our Carlos. He and the Calusa were the original protectors of our Everglades!"

Jessica added, "He needs a few more days of Florida sun to get the right skin tint. He's already got good hair, although it needs some native styling."

These conversations were background noise with little meaning for me until the reference to the Calusa rang a bell. I remembered there was a Calusa Chief called Carlos.

Carlos smiled, "I've become familiar with the work of the Climate Corps in my recent conversations with Jessica and I understand the frustrations in moving folks to more sustainable energy production. That's the problem in a democracy;

you are competing with an industry that is entrenched in an economy that does things at the expense of the environment. The profits from economic growth driven by fossil fuel power are made at the expense of middle and lower class populations. The CO_2 increase of greenhouse effect heat trapping is causing irreversible homeland loss to island and coastal societies. We need to educate and elect leaders who are able to convince others to adopt a new set of rules of economy and government. You are working hard at that and should continue. I wonder if our Colorado Community workshops might help. We have formed a network of workshops with like-minded people around the country. I suggest that such a climate workshop in this Everglades City model of transition to renewable energy might be useful. We could supplement your education and solar transition efforts."

"I suspect that many of society's decision makers have not been sufficiently concerned about the future climate to search for Orbatz' detailed presentations of the climate science. So they drift into the voting booth with little dedication to search for an environmental leader. And voters from the service industries, housekeepers, lawn and pool minders, mailpersons and UPS drivers, have had little time for environmental concern beyond the daily weather. In fact only about half of those folks even have access to the internet. This large segment of society would have considerable interest in and influence about Nature's Climate Trust if someone would lead them. Our workshops could present them with an opportunity to appreciate the part of the natural environment that the educational system has neglected. There are intelligent individuals in that service community, previously led by the political organization to support the agenda for the wealthy. We might select potential leaders of transition energy culture from that large segment of society who have been the ignorant victims of the wealthy minority engaged in business as usual. We need a few Caesar Chavez types making decisions in energy production."

I was only slightly familiar with the Community environmental workshop off the Peak-to-Peak highway in the Colorado mountains and I hadn't realized they had been active in climate change. But I had respect for Carlos' leadership activities during his time at Golden West. This sounded like an important consideration for the problems in South Florida. I was about to give this a nod when John spoke up. "I've been disappointed in reactions to the Orbatz climate science contributions. They seem to have been a necessary but not sufficient step in climate solutions. Our Climate Corps leaders haven't been able to cope with the fossil fuel industry propaganda. Perhaps someone from the grass roots would get a more active following. And there are a large number of voters in the Florida service industries who need to make intelligent decisions about climate. They might like to have a say about climate if they had someone to lead them."

Krista was giving me a hard look, but didn't bother for a reaction. "Our salt water activities in South Florida hardly compare with working in the California soil, but the climate care for our ocean is getting short shrift. I believe we could do with some help from your workshops." After a short pause, she added, "Your workshop needs a place to meet; my Island Seafood Market will contribute some goodies for meeting starters and space for formal discussions. Just say when!"

This inspired a similar thought from Jessica. "Tesla and others have supported our Climate Corps installation work at their charging stations. And their customers have discovered that these stations and the expansion of battery storage facilities to include homeowner wall units enable a mobile electric power network. Various small business outfits have found that the free solar power will bypass the expense of Florida Electric. Now the charging stations need additional hardware and we need additional financial support for this expansion. I've been working on some personal contacts to be able to invite some financial sources from Naples to a formal dinner at the Rod and Gun Club. Perhaps the additional presence of one of Carlos' Workshop Cuban leaders, and a Jim Hansen protégé, and maybe a former U.S. President, might coax some dollars for solar panels, preferably of U.S. manufacture."

The Judge had been sitting quietly during these discussions but now voiced a conclusion from these remarks. "The emergence of mobile electric competition hasn't been a serious concern for Florida Electric, but they have finally become impressed that solar energy is free once the hardware is in place. And now there is a new industry of young people active in solar panel installations and this is supporting the expansion of U.S. solar panel construction. I think our utility industries are about to realize their bottom line profit is about to move to renewals. Their procrastination would evaporate if voters would dump their political influence."

I thought to add one more supporting factor. "So we must wean Florida Electric away from political control. It could be that some pressure from workshop activities might help. A good Sandy-type storm would also stimulate some activity here. The political direction towards fossil fuel energy might abruptly disappear at the polls. I wonder if our increasing ocean source of water vapor isn't about ready to support Tropical Storm Simon."

Fishing

It was a week later that John surprised me with a knock on Krista's kitchen door as I was finishing my share of the housekeeping. "Just out exercising my bike. Thought I would check on your schedule for a backcountry fishing expedition."

"Great! It's about time. After our training episode I invested in a complete set of salt-water gear. How about finding some snook for me?"

"I had in mind a spot up the Turner River: good water and a fine place to philosophize about life. I'm not so confident about snook—you might instead try under the bridge at north end of town some evening."

"I assume we are using your whaler, but don't take me someplace without a paddle!"

"I will arrange some special embarking conditions. I would rather not have anyone with ulterior motives following us to our secret fishing hole. I will have Manny leave the whaler at the Smallwood dock on Chokoloskee tonight —I don't think they've killed anyone there recently. Then at daybreak tomorrow Luisa will drop me off there; you can safely arrive in the Prius. We may have to wade the outlet of the Turner, but we will be able to cruise up the river without observers."

The precautions were somewhat of a surprise. After a thoughtful pause I agreed. "John, I'm a bit slow, but I'm beginning to appreciate the way you live. I'll be there."

The trees were scattering the red morning sunlight as we

dropped anchor. We were sheltered under a large mahogany in deep water on an outer bend of the Turner. I was loading some 20-pound test line on my reel as John interrupted, "I'm really not too optimistic about snook, but I brought some live bait. Run your hook through the back of this little critter just below that fin—like so." John quickly had his bait on the line and was dropping it over the side. "Then adjust your bobber so he can swim a few inches off the bottom. Just let him cruise around. Then be very patient; wait until your monster with the stripe has swallowed his lunch and moved away before you set the hook. Now open your can of beer and relax."

I managed to make myself comfortable a few feet from John and made the comment, "I feel sorry for the poor baitfish trying to get off the hook."

John's reply, "You'll forget about that when you are about to sample a snook fillet, but for now you can tell me what you think of the way we are managing things in South Florida."

"Well, we seem to have properly identified the problems—Everglades destruction and sea level rise. There's not much progress on solutions though."

"Yes, those are certainly the biggies. I thought that as we enjoy our beer and this quiet environment we might give some thought to where we are on these problems. But I think it's time that we have a clear understanding of our personal outlooks. You and I have gradually moved to a close friendship and I apologize for developing our friendship without responding to your search for Orbatz. You've had some increasing reasons to suspect my identity. I'm sure my performance with the Tesla last week dissolved any remaining doubts. I am in fact that elusive Professor John Orbatz."

"John, I've recognized your subtle overtures as to that possibility, but I was just not quite certain. Thank you for clearing the air!"

He continued, "Of course you must be a bit mystified about my being able to afford the Tesla. Actually I have a sweetheart deal with the Palm Beach widow. I get to drive it as part of her project to educate the public about the fossil fuel damage to our climate. This is a cooperative venture with the electric car folks to move our transportation system from oil to solar electric. And as you no doubt observed, our neighbors have made the analysis that their old neighbor John was just pretending to be the Professor Orbatz. I hope we may leave it at that and Orbatz may continue to be an Everglades recluse."

I quickly replied, "I appreciate your desire to avoid being the target of individuals who may violently disagree with your statements and actions about our natural and social environments. You may be assured that I will not jeopardize that need."

"Russ, as you have discovered, up until last Spring I had been very vocal about my concerns about the future of the Everglades and its wildlife. In my early career, I had thought to publish an update of *River of Grass*. But I had second thoughts. This followed an event in my early career where I was fortunate to attend an American Geophysical Union research report about some measurements of atmospheric hydroxyl. That speaker introduced his talk by saying; "I felt an obligation to my GI-bill support to communicate our need to care for the environment. I thought to embed my nature messages in fictional novels. But I realized at an early date that I would fail the example of my wartime C-54 Captain to whom I had been introduced on our North Atlantic weather recon flight.

'Our Captain today is Ernie Gann; he has written *Island in the Sky,* now available as a movie.' I quickly realized that I had no hope of being so talented and successful to write for movies like that, or for books like *The High and the Mighty* and *Soldier of Fortune.* So I became a physics professor, taking measurements relating to this problem of stratospheric ozone."

John continued, "And I was convinced to abandon thoughts of becoming a famous American author or research scientist. It seemed to be a more acceptable career to stay with personal communications and pass it on in my teaching career. My recent efforts have been to explain the environmental dangers of global warming. But there was little positive response, and I deserted society to enjoy life with Luisa. I maintained a certain amount of vague identity to avoid having to worry about the possibility of unpleasant disruption of my life in the relaxed atmosphere of Everglades City. Then I began to experience some guilt when some of our young people began to worry about their South Florida future. I was gratified when the idea of the Climate Corps moved ahead, and the early successes of their work in Everglades City suggested that this might be the alternate environmental solution to the failed response of the establishment. But we are now discovering that many of our younger generation have fallen for the fossil fuel propaganda, and because of the failed educational system are ignorant of this greatest of all environmental dangers."

A persistent female mosquito distracted my initial reply. She expired in a pool of my blood. "Our Climate Corps has to do some educating. The Earth's response to global warming is much more complex than the common understanding of the prediction of a gradual increase in global temperature. A large segment of the public does not appreciate that our increasing emission of CO_2 from burning fossil fuels guarantees the additional melting of mountain glaciers and rising seas. Then there is the simple logic that the increased evaporation from the warming oceans will generate increased precipitation and energy release in extreme weather sometime, somewhere, on the Earth. Still, our increased television coverage of floods and tornadoes on the networks and weather channel is beginning to suggest a climate change relationship. But of course the fossil fuel disciples and deniers will insist that these things have always happened."

"I'm afraid you're right about the failure in dedication by our younger generation. There is a lot of fossil fuel misinformation out there. I've seen individuals in Colorado who have lost everything to a wildfire just stand and wonder how they will survive. And unsuspecting residents without flood insurance spending every minute piling up their water soaked furniture or shoveling out the mud and complaining that FEMA isn't helping. You don't really think the voters will insist that Congress enact a carbon tax and subsidize renewable energy?"

A slight pause to discourage another mosquito. "Or at best, those who actually understand the danger of burning fossil fuel are sitting on their hands waiting for someone else to fix the problem. But some of the environmental organizations have adopted the philosophy that our atmosphere is a Natural Trust that must be defended legally. Unfortunately the fossil fuel industries operate with the economic principle that the environment is there to be exploited. They fund their propaganda mill at a rate that is difficult to match by the environmental folks. And the judicial society is very slow to respond legally to the

ALEX COOK

Trust arguments. We are back to the failure of society in general to understand the science of global warming."

John agreed with my analysis. "You know, we could counter this general resistance to a carbon tax by identifying the emission penalty necessary to correct the damage to Nature's Trust, something like $40/ton of CO_2." He proceeded with another solution, "That little show at the fish market the other day was just a prelude to a big show over in Palm Beach. That wealthy widow and her friends have formed an Association of Electric Transport consisting of Teslas, Leafs, and Volts, and a collection of Priuses and assorted other hybrids. BMW and Porsche have promised to join in the near future. As you know, the Glades Restoration never got the Federal and State funding before Big Sugar began selling off to developers. We have recently learned that our Everglades buddy, the Judge, has always owned a 40-acre plot of his favorite Glades. The Electric Vehicle folks are building a display auditorium there with a seating capacity of several hundred and refreshment facility for drinks and appetizers. They may also have a heated pool for folks to enjoy before what I hope will be an inspiring sermon by Orbatz. And of course this must have a solar thermal facility with parabolic troughs to heat stuff for generating steam for the small turbines, and some to store in molten salt to keep generating power for my evening sermon. There will also be a test track for visitors to check out the vehicles. Your neighbor John will proceed from here with the vehicles; we expect several Teslas from Marco to join us. Then the full-blown Professor Orbatz will lead a formal caravan from Palm Beach to the Glades and initiate the festivities somewhat like we did at the fish market. You've seen the kind of religious programs

that are popular on the Gold Coast. We will pack them in—
and they will get the full story of global warming and climate
change."

I cautioned, "That's going to cost some big bucks, maybe
more than the widow can afford."

John explained, "Don't you imagine the electric car folks
will be delighted to get on board?"

Sounds like a whole new ballgame. This was the real
Professor Orbatz, as I had long suspected but was afraid to
hope.

My red and white bobber had ceased its aimless wander-
ing. "I think my baitfish has gone to sleep or drowned. What
now?"

"Time to shift to shrimp for sheepshead. I predict a slight
dividend increase in your tackle investment. Oh, but get a
look at our swallowtail visitor up there!"

I found an extraordinarily graceful flight of a large bird
with black edged wings and black double tail hovering over the
treetop. A sudden swoop into the branches and an apparent
need for some observation of its feet. "What's his problem?"

"He's lunching on that small lizard that he snatched out
of the tree—that reminds me, we have sandwiches Luisa sent
with us. How about a ham and cheese?"

Our fish detectors were resting quietly as we ate. Finally
John asked, "You really think our younger generation can be
effective?"

I was skeptical but hopeful, "As the Climate Corps activities mature we should see some potential leaders who can
move out into the mainstream politics. And we will have some
New Generation folks who will be ready to follow; that hasn't

been the situation in the past. Once they have the knowledge, they have some effective tools. Facebook readers could be reminded that the IPCC scientists have insisted that global warming is indeed 97% caused by human activity; the Arctic sea ice will disappear and the eventual melting of the permafrost is 99% certain. Realistically, we might hope for some successful local projects of wind and solar with a general acceptance of renewables. But there is a worrisome possibility that even this slight hesitation in warming that we accomplish with this gradual slowing of greenhouse gas emissions might be balanced by an accelerating increase of carbon dioxide and methane emissions from the permafrost and the warm coastal waters of the ocean. That is an extremely dangerous tipping point. No way will we be able to adapt to that."

"Well, I'll try to get our New Generation Climate Corps in high gear to avoid that situation." Then he became seriously dedicated. "We need an intensive campaign to identify and expose the fossil fuel disciples in government." John became increasingly optimistic. "Then perhaps our retired Senator Jamison might effectively engineer a flood of political contributions to support those identified by the Climate Corps to replace those in government who have failed to protect our environment—we must have a visit with our colleague!"

"My bobber has sunk!" And I was losing nylon from my reel.

"Wake up Russ—catch that contribution to our evening dinner!"

I was busy making a sluggish recovery of my line as John was hauling an impressive tall-bodied fish with a bony mouth into the boat. "Sheepshead!! We will have fish dinner tonight!"

Harold

My outlook on efforts to move ahead on clean energy had improved substantially after my fishing trip with John—Professor Orbatz. Time to relax and enjoy my retirement. Danny was off to school at 8 in the morning and Krista left for work a little later. It was a sunny day with clear blue sky—just the way it's supposed to be in winter in Florida. And this is the reason I had retired from the cold and wind in Colorado. Now I needed to find some entertaining way to spend my time. So I set off on my bike armed with fishing tackle for a visit to the tackle store at the boat ramp for advice and bait. Henry gave me a sympathetic smile but suggested that the fish would have been more likely to bite a few hours ago, or after sundown. I explained that I wasn't terribly concerned with prospects for a hefty catch—just wanted to sit in the sun by the water. But I needed to look as if I were doing something constructive. He said, "OK. I'll fix you up with some cut mullet and frozen shrimp. Then you can doze in the sun and maybe some stray bottom fish will eventually come along and wake you up."

So I pedaled out the causeway towards the island wearing tee shirt, shorts, and floppy straw hat, with bait and sunscreen in back pack, and rod and reel across the handlebars. I had occasionally seen fishermen near the causeway bridge so I thought I would follow suit. Too bad I couldn't have managed to bring a comfortable lawn chair. In a few minutes, I was sitting in the sand getting lathered up with UV protection.

Our wind turbine was sitting motionless and quiet in line of sight, reminding me that our attempts to convert the country to renewable energy were only a feeble step to control the Earth's greenhouse gas emissions. I began to speculate on the future climate. It was clear from the IPCC reports that business as usual was taking us down the irreversible path to a very uncomfortable climate. In fact the wind pattern had the Hadley cell dominating Florida circulation lately. I would have to seek shade in an hour or so.

But my thoughts were easily disrupted by the arrival of a big Chevy pickup that parked a few yards away. The driver secured his fishing gear and crossed the road to claim a fishing spot where the tidal current came under the bridge. I wondered if I had his usual spot—or did he know something that I didn't? But neither of our red and white bobbers exhibited any activity. My fellow fisherman stood at attention, lit his pipe, and then approached with the question, "Catching anything?"

"No, but I just arrived. Think we'll see any action?"

"Not really, but it's a pleasant place to spend some time. I believe I've seen you at the coffee house on the island. I wonder if you're like me, just enjoying the sun without having to shovel snow."

"Good guess. And you're retired—from where?"

"I'm Harold. I used to run a small construction outfit in northern Illinois. When business fell off because folks couldn't afford a mortgage for a new house, I convinced my wife that I needed to go fishing. We have a mobile home on the island. Now she insists that I get out of the house so she can sit and watch TV. So I sit around out here and sometimes catch a fish—nothing worth cleaning to eat though. My main accomplishment is a couple of tender red spots on my cheeks."

"I think that's a Florida story that's been published a few times." I lifted a finger for a pause and offered my tube of sunscreen.

Harold waved a hand, "I always put it on at home—I guess it just doesn't work after a couple of hours." After a couple of puffs on his pipe, he queried, "You're from up north someplace?"

"Right, and I am Russ. Retired from a small college in Colorado. Used to teach history—getting interested in climate change now."

"Ah, yes. Been wondering about that but don't hear or see much about it."

"Right. You just about have to search on the internet. The website by Orbatz in the Everglades is an excellent start. The human increase in greenhouse gases like carbon dioxide and methane is a problem that we need to change, but there's not much public attention or voter activity. And the coal and oil money convinces the politicians looking to get elected that they should ignore it."

"But apparently the locals here think it's important enough to go for renewables with that big wind turbine out there and this line of solar panels along the causeway."

"Yes, there's a Climate Corps of young people who know it will affect their future. And there was a float of cash that helped it along. But it's proving to be an uphill battle to make this a general solution for much of the country. And the scientists say that there is no way we can go back to a normal climate."

Harold replied, "I know—that's scary! So what will it take to get this country—and the rest of the world—to realize we've got a common problem that we need to work together on before we all go down the tube?" Then he surprised me with, "Since we didn't pay for dumping that CO_2 in the air by generating power with coal, I suppose we should expect to pay a little more for pretty solar panels, nice big wind turbines, and maybe some extra safe nuclear reactors. But none of us wants to do that because we're basically greedy."

Harold tilted his head up about 30 degrees in the general direction of the Yucatan and waved the hand not holding his pipe from Texas to Panama. "This atmosphere is not mine or yours; it's used by every plant and animal on the planet. It's something we hold in common, yours to breathe and mine to smoke my pipe. If it is abused for whatever profit, we will all suffer. Looks like we have the Tragedy of the Commons all over again!" He shifted hands on the pipe and vented some of his frustration by skipping a horseshoe crab shell across the bay.

As the ripples diminished, I replied, "It's discouraging I know. Our generation's attitude is hopeless. But there is a movement for change in our New Generation Climate Corps." I explained, "Our young people have adopted the philosophy that our planet's environment constitutes a Nature's Trust that must be legally protected. But the courts have not yet accepted this concept. The general public must respond to this change in attitude."

"But when will that happen?" Harold continued, "I have to wonder if the aggressive exploitation of the environment and competition for material wealth by us humans are genetic traits that will prevent my generation from moving to a sustainable civilization." With that pessimistic thought, Harold recharged his pipe and trudged back to sit quietly at his fishing site.

A ring-billed gull landed gracefully on the sand a few yards away. It had that optimistic patient stance as it waited for a choice fragment of my waterlogged bait. I returned to my cautious optimistic stare at the red and white bobber that was responding suggestively to the ripples generated by the Chokoloskee breeze. The blades of the wind turbine began to turn, but ever so slowly.

EPILOGUE

Colorado

I must first tell you of the further disasters in my beloved Rocky Mountains. Wildfires in the urban-forest interface in Colorado had been on the increase with global warming.

The above average temperatures in the warm dry June days in advance of the summer monsoon were extremely aggravated by the loss of water to the flatland farms and cities. The dry lightning fires of the foothills were beginning to occur in the high country.

The USFS in the Front Range hoped to decrease firefighting costs and score points with mountain residents by removing beetle-killed trees and beginning advanced wildfire mitigation. But it was business as usual for the bureaucracy of the USFS. Clearcut fuelbreaks were awarded to the highest bidder of the timber industry's big machines. They ignored the CSFS-citizen thinning demonstration where the slash was chipped by the locals and returned to the forest. The timber people clearcut the thinned healthy lodgepole pines, and that slash was now stacked for burning, leaving the forest floor free of nutrients, and open to wind driven evaporation.

The late afternoon lightning strikes on the tall lodgepoles of the residual lodgepole forest moved into the brushy undergrowth and down and dead of the ravines, deemed inconvenient to process by the timber people and ignored by the USFS. The dry-season downslope wind produced a wall of wildfire into the foothills. Then when the windstorm generated by the fire took control, the fire moved back up the mountain into virgin forest. The fuel of the homeowner-neglected defensible zones insured the huge explosions of expensive mansions. But a small A-frame surrounded by aspens and thinned lodgepoles sat unscathed, surrounded by blackened forest. This raging inferno continued for weeks until much of the Front Range Forest was blackened.

The summer monsoon began to answer the mountain residents' plea, "But we need the moisture!" A new atmospheric circulation regime had been initiated by the enhanced warming of the Arctic. The weather began a repeat of the 1000-year flood of September 2013. The upslope precipitation began on the fire blackened east slope of the Front Range. Afternoon thunderstorms of increased frequency became virtually continuous for 10 days. The fire-baked soil resisted any addition to the groundwater and the ashes formed a dike just above the abrupt drop from the high country to the foothills. On the 11th day the deluge sent a wall of mud down every canyon from Clear Creek to the Cache la Poudre. Every flood plain to and including the South Platte was left with an 18-inch gummy deposit. Unwary residents watched from rooftops for National Guard rescue copters; numerous houses were unwillingly relocated to Nebraska. The Weather Channel photos of the mountain damage and predictions of extreme weather contributed to Krista's continued reticence for a return trip West.

The fossil fuel industries continued to sacrifice humanity's future on planet Earth in order to insure their profits. Citizens of the Sunshine State accepted this philosophy of economic greed and ignored any thoughts of mitigation of greenhouse gas emission control. Efforts by The New Generation Climate Corps to explain the consequences of the CO_2 enhanced atmospheric greenhouse effect were met with apathy, and their grassroots demonstrations of climate change solutions stalled. The predictions of extreme weather by the IPCC were beginning to materialize.

Tesla II Transition

B ack in the subtropical paradise of South Florida, I found that the natives had been convinced to concentrate on preparations for adaptation to the inconveniences of sea level rise and occasional cat 5 hurricanes. Thoughts of mitigation of the cause of climate change were frowned upon; political leaders forbade its mention. The electric utilities had responded to the potential competition of homeowner solar investments with utility owned solar gardens where space was available. But the homeowner associations in South Florida frowned on roof mounted solar panels and every inch of land was in the hands of developers.

The electric car advances in Palm Beach were not anticipated. Solar powered electric cars were becoming increasingly popular. Solar powered charging stations became readily available along I-95. Free energy was available for luxury cars and the small electric taxis supplementing light rail transport, with hardware purchased by the new auto industry and installation of solar panels contracted for by the Climate Corps. This had also expanded into a bootlegged free mobile source of electrical power as stored energy was simply transferred to the homeowners' wall battery units. While Florida Electric did not view this practice as serious competition, the emergence of expanded industries of solar panel construction and installation had inspired the utility to build more solar gardens. They had begun to appreciate the free solar energy advantage in their economy.

There was new social activity in the Glades, inspired by the Tesla, BMW, and Porsche electric cars. The solar powered Transport Future facility was in full swing with televised messages warning of the evil of the climate change temptations of the fossil fuel industries. The New Generation Climate Corps was proud to introduce their champion, Professor John Orbatz, to discuss the opportunity for modern electric vehicle transportation in this era of rapid climate change. He reminded the audiences that the business communities of South Florida had especially welcomed those retirees who were able to demonstrate their business successes. He accused them, "It is understandable that you have resisted any perturbations to your retirement arrangements. You have adapted to climate change to maintain a luxurious lifestyle but have ignored the need to mitigate the fossil fuel cause of the accelerating global warming. And our society has adopted a business as usual attitude that leaves the low income service community oblivious to the problem."

Orbatz explained the unpleasant fact that, "Nevertheless, the atmospheric greenhouse effect that has given us a favorable climate is responding to our wanton pollution of increasing the carbon dioxide that is the control knob on the thermal trapping by water vapor. This energy imbalance is driving the melting of mountain glaciers and polar ice, and the rising sea levels, and increases of extreme weather episodes. We have initiated a dangerous climate change."

"We must accept the destruction of our coastal urban environments, and the return of our land to the sea. We will no longer be able to obtain fresh water from our salt infiltrated aquifers or grow food in the depleted everglades muck that is now in danger of saltwater inundation. Human society, as well as the native birds and animals, must abandon South Florida in the very near future."

The wealthy in the audience ignored this analysis, not pertinent in their lifetimes. But the middle class parents were surprised and their offspring were shocked. In the succeeding Orbatz lectures, the service communities filled the audience; this was their sole source of climate information. The wealthy were absent. A movement was underway with parents from a Boca Raton middle school, cooperating with the New Generation Climate Corps, to begin legal steps against the criminal action of elected officials and their fossil fuel supporters in their willful damage of the atmospheric structure of Nature's Trust. This was made more urgent by the appearance of a very large Midatlantic tropical storm.

Saturday afternoon excursions to the Transport Future featured stone crab claws from Krista along with gin and tonic. The top ocean research experts from Virginia Key continued to arrive with warnings of the decreasing good fortunes from the sea. And the social evenings in Palm Beach had become increasingly delicate in discussions with the fossil fuel advocates for electric power generation.

Simon

In Everglades City we had survived the minor inundations of several tropical storms of an extended subtropical summer season, and had made war on the mosquitoes. We were lucky. The Miami Beach residents at 4 ft mean sea level had been using kayaks, rowboats, and bill-fisherman charter boats to move about in the twice-daily high tides that inundated the streets. And very recently they were experiencing a continuous 3 ft sea level encroachment generated by a huge tropical storm a thousand miles out in the Atlantic. Their urgent request for expenditure of adaptation funds was stalled by Congressional concerns of economic damage to business as usual. NOAA's predicted track of the developing storm was for it to move slowly through the Bahamas and follow the Gulf Stream northward offshore from Miami to Long Island.

As we in Everglades City monitored the approach of the huge Atlantic storm, it became obvious that our east-coast neighbors in South Florida were about to lose their homes. Category 3 Hurricane Simon approached Miami Beach in early August with torrential rains in addition to a 10 ft storm surge. The eye lingered over the Gulf Stream but the downpour and strong winds extended deep into the Florida peninsula. Residents of seaside condominiums refused to move as usual, but their air conditioning, entertainment and grocery deliveries failed with the shut down of the Turkey Point nuclear reactors.

The less wealthy non-white service communities were screaming ineffectively for FEMA assistance in evacuating. The Miccosukees began constructing tent-modified chickees along the Tamiami Trail for the Cuban evacuees. Convoys of vegetable laden trucks from Immokalee began to supply food to the Tamiami Trail city. As the line of chickees approached Everglades City, Krista's fishing fleet accepted donations for fuel as they worked nonstop to supply seafood to the refugees.

The tourist trade at Island Seafood had dwindled to an occasional cluster of disaster gawkers, but the locals continued to depend on their dinner seafood. I was drafted to a few odd jobs that Krista thought I might safely handle. John and Luisa's shopping visit brought an atmosphere of serious concern. He began with a casual remark that identified the Orbatz of environmental authority. When I quizzed him, "What's up, Prof?" he confided, "I've just had some e-mail conversations with one of our satellite analysts over in Miami. She has some preliminary observations on the slowing of the Gulf Stream that are worrisome. Perhaps you are familiar with its role in the thermohaline circulation. The Stream's surface water in the Arctic gets cold and loaded with salt so that it sinks and forms a deep ocean return circulation. The recent satellite measurements suggest a slowing of the Gulf Stream that may be caused by a fresh rainwater dilution of the cold return water and stagnation of the sinking return. This could diminish the warm climate of northern European countries. It would also cause an increased pooling of warm Atlantic surface water. This has always been expected sometime in the future, but this is a surprisingly early development."

I stared at this sober faced Orbatz. "Do you suppose this will change the storm behavior in the Atlantic? Maybe even Simon?"

"Hard to say. And of course the climate deniers and politicians and the CSU hurricane forecasters will insist that Simon is just a temporary demonstration of a normal hurricane season. But we should be giving more serious attention to large-scale adaptations. Our mitigation efforts are already too late."

"Actually I've been wondering what will happen to this Trail chickee settlement. Maybe it's time to think about an organized migration of coastal folks up to the ridge in mid-Florida just past the Big-O."

Orbatz gave this thought long consideration. "We need to increase our emphasis on mitigation to get control of the greenhouse gases. But I believe we should also get the Climate Corps on board with some serious study of the relocation of our coastal cities. We will need the experts at the University to make some sense of the situation and give some weight to counter the political resistance."

"Maybe Simon will help with a wake-up call."

Simon grew to a cat 5 and moved slowly along the East Coast northward to the Orlando area with a 12 ft storm surge and 16 in per day rainfall. Florida residents were about to be reminded that they must begin to pay the piper for the consequences of what they thought was the cheap energy in the past. Luxurious single-family houses extending westward to the Turnpike suffered irreparable damage with stubborn residents bailing water from evacuation centers. The deluge of rainfall overwhelmed the Drainage District arrangements for flood control. The Everglades River of Grass became an 18-inch deep torrent moving through the eastern Glades to Shark River and Florida Bay, scouring the area of the pollutants of residential areas and Big Sugar Agriculture. Everglades National Park and Florida Bay became the septic tank for South Florida developments. The Overseas Highway was impassable with high tides and the Florida Keys of the Conch Republic became dependent on Cuban supplies. The Florida subtropical paradise was in big trouble.

The global warming sea level increase had brought a gradual influx of brackish water into the Western Glades along the Tamiami Trail. This climate change was monitored briefly each February by the devout pilgrimage of a pair of faithful snowbirds from the Colorado mountains. The gentleman leaning slightly on the slender cypress hiking staff was always attired in jeans and flannel shirt with the additions of black hat, bow tie, and hiking boots. His lady companion wore dark glasses and copious sun protection as she caressed the massive head of the attentive Landseer Newfoundland. They found a new mangrove forest efficiently replacing the dying pond cypress.

ABOUT THE AUTHOR

Alex Cook is the pen name of Clyde R. Burnett, Emeritus Professor of Physics from Florida Atlantic University with over 50 years intermittent experience in the Everglades environment. He currently lives in the Colorado mountains near the NOAA Fritz Peak Atmospheric Observatory, where he has secured 33 years of measurements of atmospheric hydroxyl, where he has secured 33 years of measurements of atmospheric hydroxyl, related to the problem of stratospheric ozone depletion (www.stratospheric-hydroxyl.com). He has recently given attention to the science of global warming-climate change. He is the author of *The Greenhouse Effect-A Legacy, Jason and the Grizzly, The Family Guide to Disruptive Climate Change,* and *The Community,* novels with global warming-climate change embedded, and the nonfiction *Nature's Greenhouse: Ominous Developments.*